D1327054

A

THE ARROW
AND TWO OTHER STORIES

THE ARROW

and

Two Other Stories

by

CHRISTOPHER MORLEY

LONDON
WILLIAM HEINEMANN, LTD.
1927

Printed in Great Britain at
The Westminster Press
411A Harrow Road
London, W. 9

CONTENTS

PLEASED TO MEET YOU

B

I

" I NEVER supposed it would come to this," said Frau Innsbruck. Her vigorous torso, tightly compressed in black, creaked a little with indignation.

The small sunny chamber where they lunched together showed nothing to suggest what deplorable condition " this " was. But it seemed to be something she saw through the window. From that outlying wing of the old building they could look across a well-trimmed lawn to the façade of the chateau. Over the roof of mossed crumbling tiles and conical towers floated a green and white banner which had just been raised.

" How are we to behave when he arrives," she continued, " and what are we to call him? Why, the man started life as a fishmonger. I never thought we'd see such doings in the Farniente Palace."

Her companion breathed heavily over the last of his roll and honey. Herr Romsteck was elderly, portly, and austere; his manner showed that he knew any attempt to express his feelings would be inadequate. A blob of honey had fallen on the lapel of his worn but

3

immaculate tail coat. He removed it half-heartedly, as though such trifles hardly mattered now.

" It isn't a palace any longer," he said. " I had orders this morning from the Commissioner of Public Buildings—think of that, Public Buildings—that from now on this is officially known as the Executive Mansion. The Council of the League of Nations does not desire that any ' reactionary ' sentiment be retained in our government names."

" What *right*, I should like to know, has the League of Nations to interfere? " exclaimed the housekeeper. " League of Nations indeed! League of Barbarians! Do you know that when all those foreigners were here, English prime ministers and people like that, one of them actually smoked a pipe in his bedroom—the very room that was Duchess Liesel's boudoir. Oh, I know it is even harder for you, whose family have served here with honour for generations. But I thought that when the horrible war was over things would be better; and we've come to this. We might as well be a soviet."

" We shall have to be on our dignity," said Romsteck. " The future of Illyria is in our hands. It is the grand dukes and generals and statesmen, perhaps even the fishmongers, who get into the history books; but *we* are the real power behind the throne. It is we who see that their meals are suitably planned, their beds aired, their trousers ironed, their social precedences arranged. By sheer excellence of example we shall have to lift this unfortunate proletarian above his natural depravity. Let me point out to you also, it is dangerous to speak lightly of the League of Nations. They might have wiped us off the map altogether."

"Ah, the good old days," sighed Innsbruck. "The Grand Duke with his Rolls Royce and his beautiful ladies and the laughter on the terrace. There was some satisfaction in serving in an elegant and vicious household like that. There was no talk then of economies and republics and debts. The bourgeois virtues are so dull."

There was a tap at the door and Karl the wine-steward came in. He was a grizzled little fellow in a green felt apron stained by years of grubbing among cobwebs and mildew.

"Your pardon, Herr Romsteck," he said, "but here is the cellar inventory you wanted. We are a bit short in the Burgundies; when the envoys from Geneva were here they absolutely demolished the 1911 Chambertin and Hospice de Beaune. The Musigny also is very low."

"The gentlemen from the League," observed Romsteck, "have a very genteel taste in wine."

"Except the Americans. When the American

5

commissioner was here to arrange our finances he would have nothing but champagne. However I worked off a cheap sparkling Chablis on him and he did not know the difference."

"Considering the habits of our late lamented Grand Duke," said the major-domo, looking over the list, " your bins seem to be very fairly stocked."

" Plenty good enough, anyhow, for a republican administration. What a calamity! "

" It is a time of crisis," said Romsteck gravely. " There must be no nonsense about retrenchment or we shall all find ourselves retrenched out of existence. We are lucky to be here at all."

" Yes," cried Karl, " and what did it? If I had not had presence of mind to serve the 1865 cognac the evening the protocol was signed, we should have been annexed to Italy. I saw the hard hearts of those premiers begin to soften after the third glass."

" I hope you have plenty of it left," said Frau Innsbruck bitterly. " There may be need of it."

" But do you suppose there will be anyone in this new government who will appreciate the finer things? " There was the wistfulness of the connoisseur in the cellarer's voice. " These proletarians, will they have a taste for anything beyond beer? "

" We shall educate them," said Romsteck.

" The tradition of our vanished aristocracy rests with *us*."

The door opened, admitting Pigalle, the chef, the only member of the staff who considered himself privileged to enter the major-domo's sitting-room without knocking. His tall white cap was furiously awry, his face engraved with irony.

" I see the flag of the republic has been raised," he said grimly. " Our chief magistrate arrives to-day. Pigs' trotters and sauer kraut, I conceive, will be delicacies adequate to this evening's repast."

" Pigalle," said Romsteck, " my heart bleeds for you. I know the suffering of the great creator confronted by patrons unworthy of his art. But a word with you in all gravity. We face a situation unparalleled. It is not with pigs' trotters and sauer kraut that we can raise this new ministry to a sense of national dignity. None knows better than you the elevating influence of cultivated fare. It is with truffled quails or a turbot boiled in wine that we will strike the proper note."

" On this new budget you allow me ! " exclaimed the chef. "Absurd ! Besides I thought it best to refrain from fish. It might be considered an allusion."

" You, who are master of your art, will know best how to proceed," said Romsteck tactfully. " Strike terror into their hearts with the delicacy of your cuisine. It is the subtlest form of revenge."

"It is true," said the chef, "that my truffled quails *au basilic*, and a Strasbourg pâté in the shape of a prostrate nymph, did much to mollify the tyrants from Geneva. I attribute it to that pâté that we were not annexed to Jugo-slavia."

"It may well be," said Romsteck. "And now, since the Herr President will soon be here, I think we should call the staff together and say a few words in regard to the etiquette we will pursue. Frau Innsbruck, if you will have the household assembled in the great hall I shall address them briefly."

II

THE traveller in Illyria, whether a casual
sightseer or one of the various commis-
sioners, diplomats, and errants of fortune who
found themselves there during the compli-
cations of After-War, has gazed through the
high iron gates on the Pannonia Platz and
admired the Farniente Palace at the end of its
avenue of linden trees. Built long ago by a
French architect for an Adriatic millionaire
and occupied for generations by Austrian
minor princes, it stands islanded in the loop
of a little river and looks over the old city
toward the opal horizon of the Carinthian
alps. The town has the polyglot and cosmo-
politan flavour appropriate to a region that
has been a debatable ground among rival
powers since the time of the Ostrogoths. The
prime ministers and economic experts of the
great powers carved out the republic of Illyria
from the relics of a fallen empire and encouraged the newly risen Labour Party to put
one of its leaders in the chair as first President.
They came from Geneva to Farniente, spread
maps and agenda papers over the departed
Grand Duke's vast dining-table, and (as we

9

have heard) polished off what was left of the Grand Duke's pre-War Burgundies. They allotted the infant republic a generous quota of war debts to pay, arranged for a bond issue and a loan from an American banker, and impressed upon the anxious parliament the necessity of a convincing show of republican enthusiasm. They spoke sternly of order, productivity, and a prompt stabilization of the florin. Then they departed, without having given much thought to the possible social embarrassments of the new President. They had more urgent matters to wrestle with, and all they wanted for the time being was to hear as little of Illyria as possible.

But these problems were sharply present to Herr Guadeloupe as he and his daughter Nyla drove in a rickety taxi to take up official residence in the palace he had never entered and which had been, only a few months before, so far beyond the horizon of his most fantastic dreams. The fishmongering that Frau Innsbruck resented was long in the past, but he remained what he had always been, a simple sturdy little man with the conscientious bonhomie of his peasant stock. He was quite aware that only the comedy of circumstance had thrust him into this position, and that both extremes of Illyrian politics would rejoice at his humiliation and downfall. He was correspondingly eager to tread softly and not make mistakes. There had been a great meeting of his supporters the night before, at which glowing forecasts were made of what the new republic would mean for the labouring classes. The *New Freedom* and the *Folkvoice*, very ill-printed proletarian journals, had come out with predictions which he knew were fallacious. A demonstration had been planned to celebrate his move to the palace. To avoid this uncomfortable publicity he sent out Nyla, two hours before the time advertised, to call a cab. They slipped away from the modest home where Nyla had kept house for her widowed father. Now, in an elderly vehicle of Detroit lineage, they came clanking solemnly down the famous alley of lime trees.

Nyla, a handsome spirited girl of nineteen, was naturally elated.

" Now, Father," she said gaily, " you mustn't be nervous. Everything will be all right. Don't push your hat over one eye like that."

Guadeloupe fidgeted unhappily in the new outfit of cutaway coat and wing collar which she had insisted on his buying. Nyla had carefully observed the British foreign minister when that handsome creature was in Farniente, and had planned the President's attire on the same lines. It was less successful on his short thick figure. His hands flitted instinctively in search of his pipe, but the arrangement of pockets in a cutaway coat was unfamiliar.

" I *am* nervous," he said, and began to pull off his gloves.

" Nonsense! Anyone who can talk to political meetings as you can needn't be afraid. You mustn't forget that you're a great man. Don't you dare take off those gloves until I tell you. How all this would have surprised Mother."

He relapsed into dogged and wary silence. " Political meetings are easy," he reflected, " but this social racket is something quite different. If we're our natural selves, the aristocrats will sneer; if we put on airs, the populace will resent it." He thought wistfully of the little home where he and Nyla had been so comfortable.

The taxi-driver, a fiercely moustached and emotional mountaineer, was enormously excited at having been chosen to drive Illyria's first President to the palace. This would be something to talk about for the rest of his life. His sense of the dignity of the occasion suggested a slow and stately progress with much unnecessary tooting on an old rubber bulb horn. This attracted a dog of no importance who was sunning in the broad Pannonia Platz. With a quick instinct for the unusual he accompanied the car down the sacred *allée*. bounding and yapping just under the fender.

" Tell the driver not to go so slow," Nyla said as they approached. " It looks more like a funeral than a President arriving. Oh see, Daddy, there's the new flag, the flag of the Republic. I'm so thrilled! "

" It *will* be a funeral, if that dog doesn't look out," said Herr Guadeloupe.

The driver, adjured to move faster, rather overdid it. He shot across the stone bridge, spun round the curved driveway, pulled up at the broad front steps with a squeal of brakes and sliding of tires on the gravel. Behind them the dog, one of whose feet had been caught by surprise, yelled insult and reproach.

" Sit still," said Nyla hastily. " Probably there'll be a footman or somebody to open the door."

But the Executive Mansion seemed strangely deserted. The big doorway stood closed. The agitated taxi-man also remained nervously in his seat, afraid of doing something wrong.

" What do we do next? " said Herr Guadeloupe.

After a brief hesitation they got out, the taxi-man seized the Presidential portfolio, and they stood anxiously on the steps.

" Good God, I don't see any door-bell."

" Now, Father, don't get rattled. We've got a right to be here."

" I knew something like this would happen. If it gets into the papers——"

13

The driver was peering through the pane of the door.

" Why, there's the whole crowd of 'em inside there," he said hoarsely. " Shall I bang on the glass? "

" For heaven's sake don't," exclaimed Nyla.

But he was not going to miss his chance of a lifetime to create a sensation. Already he had opened the door and thrust his head in. Romsteck, not expecting the arrival so early, was just finishing his speech to the assembled household. They were all there, footmen, chambermaids, cooks, gardeners, sentries, the whole staff of the palace, receiving their instructions. They stood respectfully grouped while Romsteck, on the third tread of the grand staircase, was explaining the ethics of domestic service under a republic.

" Hey, wake up there! " shouted the taximan. " Here's the President."

III

TO Herr Guadeloupe, who was accustomed to the primitive ministrations of one peasant maid, it was hardly credible that these were all servants. For an instant, seeing so unexpectedly large a gathering, the notion occurred to him that this was a conspiracy of die-hard royalists, met for some final desperation in honour of the old regime. But Romsteck, advancing with episcopal mien, was a reassuring figure; so impressive indeed that the embarrassed President at first imagined him some dignitary of the League of Nations, left behind to supervise the installation. For the League he had a wholesome horror, having learned that all its dealings cost him toil and responsibility. There was no knowing when the Paris-Constantinople Express might not drop off, at the junction a few miles away, another committee of gentlemen with brief-cases empowered to look into Illyrian affairs.

"Welcome, Herr President," said Romsteck solemnly. "You find the staff assembled to do you honour. I am the major-domo."

"How do you do, Major?" said Guadeloupe nervously. He removed his hat and bowed formally. Straightening again he found a tall figure in uniform holding out a hand, which he grasped with grateful cordiality.

" Your hat, Herr President," Romsteck explained.

The President tried to catch Nyla's eye, to know whether the time had come to remove his gloves.

" My gloves, Major. That is, I mean, my daughter."

" The Fraülein is worthy of this ancient house's tradition of beauty," said Romsteck gallantly. " I present Frau Innsbruck, the housekeeper."

" Also worthy of the ancient tradition," said the flustered President. Then, noticing the lady's age, he attempted to improve on the remark. " We shall cohabit in friendly tranquillity, I'm sure."

" The Herr President does me too much honour," said Frau Innsbruck.

" Don't forget to pay the taxi," Nyla whispered in his ear.

A gloved hand is awkward in rummaging a trouser pocket. It came out with some bank-notes but also with the toothbrush which he had remembered at the last moment.

" My luggage," he began.

" It shall be well cared for, Herr President. If you will entrust it——"

Another open palm was ready; this time he

knew enough not to shake it, but gave it the toothbrush instead. It was borne ceremoniously away.

" I mean to say my luggage will be here presently."

" The Herr President's portfolio," said the taxi-man officiously, coming forward with the brief-case, to which he had obstinately clung.

" Pardon, Major, but have you any change? " Herr Guadeloupe, thriftily examining his money, could find nothing less than a fifty florin note. It suddenly occurred to him to wonder whether Presidents have expense accounts. This was a point that had not been covered by the constitutionalists from Geneva.

" Health and happiness to the new Republic," ejaculated the taxi-man, " and perhaps at such a moment the Herr President——"

" I will arrange the matter," said Romsteck severely.

Frau Innsbruck was already escorting Nyla upstairs, and the anxious statesman felt free to discard his gloves. He was more terrified than cheered by the grave politeness of the unknown official. All his democratic instincts prompted him to suggest some little friendly celebration. He felt an immense eagerness to catch all these observant eyes with a cordial nod; he would have liked to make a short speech on the future of Illyria and follow it by treating to a drink all round. In the rustic meetings to which he was best accustomed this would have been enormously successful, but this company of maids in neat uniforms and footmen in white cotton stockings was an audience he did not understand. He was clearing his throat to make some general salutation when Romsteck advanced upon him sombrely with a whisk brush and dusted off his coat.

" The Herr President's trousers," he said sharply, and a footman knelt down to re-arrange the drape of those garments.

" I'm afraid they're too long," said the President bashfully. " Please, Major, do not trouble yourself—I must shorten my suspenders." He looked round unhappily, almost fearing they would insist on his doing so immediately.

" The Grand Duke always liked to have his trousers adjusted when he came in from out-doors," said Romsteck.

" I believe I arrived sooner than you expected."

" It is of no consequence," said Romsteck. " Your apartments are in readiness. Now, Herr President, if you please I will conduct you through the mansion." He gave a sign of dismissal, and the attendants dispersed. The younger chambermaids, who had been on the verge of nervous titters, fled hurriedly to talk it over. Guadeloupe wiped his forehead.

" You are very kind," he said. " This, you will understand, is something of an ordeal."

They stood in the great paved hall, where the beautiful stone stair, with its wrought-iron balustrade, runs up to a gallery overhead. Along the wall hung portraits of old seventeenth-century Dukes of Farniente. The President had hardly realized yet that he was actually going to live in this place. He felt more like a visitor in a museum.

" I always wondered what the palace was like inside," he said politely. " It must be difficult to keep warm in winter."

" This is the Red Room," announced Romsteck, leading the way to an adjoining chamber. "This escritoire of rosewood and mother-of-pearl was a masterpiece of the great Venetian cabinet-maker Belluno. The tapestry, with the monogram of the Hapsburgs, was given to the palace by the Emperor Maximilian. In this room the Grand Duke used to meet his ministers for business discussions, mainly to increase the taxes. Behind these curtains was where the anarchist concealed himself when he fired at the Grand Duke Moritz. You see, there is plenty of space for an assassin to hide." With a dramatic air he pulled the hangings aside. Guadeloupe was relieved to observe that the embrasure was empty. He wondered whether he and his cabinet could successfully discuss the rehabilitation of the florin—a subject involving much lively argument—sitting on those fragile gilt chairs.

"On this other side," continued the major-domo, throwing open large glass doors, " is the grand salon. It overlooks the terrace and the rose garden. The stream, you notice, runs just beneath. We call it a moat, but of course it is really the river."

" There ought to be good fishing," said Guadeloupe cheerfully. " I dare say there are carp in that water. I could catch one for supper some day. A carp, stuffed with chest-nuts, is very good eating."

Romsteck tactfully avoided the subject of fish. " The carved panels over the mantel," he pointed out, " have three bullet holes, which have been carefully retained as a sou-venir of the revolution in '48. This is known as the Blue Room; here you will receive the representatives of foreign governments. The American commissioner, for instance, desir-ing to know when the next instalment will be paid."

The President skidded a little on the po-lished floor, but followed his guide without comment.

"At the north end of the palace, adjoining the tower, is the ballroom. In the north tower is the Purple Room. There the Grand Duke used to entertain specially favoured ladies."

The President brightened a little.

" There was once an underground passage from the cellar of the tower, beneath the moat, to a summer-house in the park. It was there that the Duke escaped during the Terror."

" I hope it is still open," said Guadeloupe.

" The Yellow Room, a small parlour painted with cupids, is between the ballroom and the salon. The Duke used to play cards there after dinner. The American ambassador often came down from Vienna to play poker with him."

" I think I have heard that the Duke was unlucky at cards," said the President.

" To be in debt to America is quite in the Farniente tradition," remarked the other. " The Dukes of Illyria always led lives full of romantic hazard. There is hardly a chamber in the palace that has not been the scene of some deed of violence. In the state dining-room the crystal chandelier is chipped; that happened when His Grace was attacked by a demented footman who disliked his table manners. Beyond the dining-room is the billiard-room, and past that, in the south tower, the Dark Room."

" The Dark Room? Was the Duke a photographer? "

" He had a hobby that way. Not all his exposures were in the most delicate taste. It used to be His Grace's boast that in a different

21

walk of life he could have prospered as a merchant of Parisian postal cards. In fact, very likely that is what he is doing now. But this is called the Dark Room with a double significance. It was there that Prince Oscar was murdered. They laid out the body on this billiard-table."

The President was growing a little weary. He had had a difficult morning, and in the stress of packing and getting off he had gone without lunch.

" I suppose, Major," he suggested politely, " there is a room where we might sit down with a glass of beer and a pipe? "

" The Grand Duke, at this hour of the afternoon, would sometimes take a cup of tea, in the English fashion," said Romsteck firmly. " But he never smoked. His laxities, if I may be so candid, were quite of another sort. The British ambassador, who occasionally came here to play tennis, was encouraged to confine his pipe to the garden."

Herr Guadeloupe had less than no enthusiasm for tea, but he dared not demur.

" It is kind of you, Major, to put me wise to these matters. I trust you will sit down with us and enjoy a cup. When must you return to Geneva? "

" To Geneva? " exclaimed Romsteck. " I have never visited Geneva."

" Oh? Well, then, which of the Great Powers do you represent? "

" And still I can't make him out," Guadeloupe complained to his daughter when he finally escaped upstairs to wash and prepare himself for tea. " If he's a major why doesn't he wear uniform? And how was I to know who he was? I thought he must be at least another Lloyd George."

" Never you mind, Daddy," she consoled him. " Isn't it all *wonderful*? It's like living in a fairy tale."

" Like living in a cemetery," he said morosely. " I've seen the places where all the Dukes were murdered or shot at."

" Wait till I get hold of that solemn old creature," she cried gaily. " I'll teach him not to bully you. And what do you think? I have a maid to look after me, a darling, called Lorli. And a bathroom all to myself—did you ever *hear* of such a thing? "

" Why, so have I," exclaimed the President, exploring. " It must be mine, for they've put my toothbrush here. Private bathrooms. Good heavens, they always said the Duke was a libertine, it must have been true."

IV

BUT Nyla's confidence abated when she found that she had to pour the tea—a beverage little drunk in Illyria—with two footmen standing attentively beside her. If they had not been there she could have studied and probably solved the complicated array of jugs, dishes, napkins, spirit lamps and other utensils; but those watchful figures frightened her. The obvious course was to use some of everything, and her father sat innocently drinking from a cup that contained both cream and lemon, unaware that this would have grieved the British Foreign Office. There was a generous assortment of rich but flimsy sandwiches and pastries, but the hungry President, conscious of scrutiny, was too uneasy to do them justice. He sat some distance from the source of supply, with an anxious feeling that it would be unseemly to shift his chair. Each tidbit was less than a square mouthful, so the alert flunkeys were busy offering him a constant succession of dishes. He sipped in silence until the lemon, gradually warring against the cream, became unbearable.

"George," he said, "take this away and drink it for me. Don't tell that Major or he'll get me into trouble with the British government."

It required both servants, apparently, to remove the offending cup. When they had left the room Guadeloupe hitched his chair nearer the table and seized several sandwiches at once.

"I'll bet they've got some grand food in the pantry," he said dismally, "if I could only get at it. You know, this won't do. If any of the Labour members saw us in a lay-out like this, I'd be impeached.—What do you suppose we'll get for supper?" He thought sadly of the old kitchen in their vacated home in the Hirschgasse, the shining copper pots ranged on the mantel above the tile stove, the larder that he always raided late at night.

"I wonder," he added, "if there's any chance of onion soup?"

For twenty years Herr Guadeloupe had had onion soup for supper almost every evening. In fact in his electoral campaign onion soup had become almost a political symbol. The cartoonists had seized upon it as an emblem of solid proletarian thrift and the traditional Illyrian simplicities. Drawings of Herr Guadeloupe dipping in his tureen and puffing his pipe, first intended for ridicule, had proved to be advantageous. The Labour

Party had been borne to power, in a manner of speaking, on a tide of onion soup.

"We may as well find out," said Nyla. "And, Daddy, you must remember they probably call it *dinner*, and it won't be until late, seven o'clock I dare say."

Summoned by the footmen, Romsteck appeared. He looked specially austere as he had not expected to be interrupted just then. He and Frau Innsbruck had just sat down to compare notes over a private glass of beer. The President put away his unlit pipe, which he had been fingering hopefully, and rose politely from his chair.

"Pardon me, Major, for disturbing you. I just wished to know, so I can make my calculations, what time will supper be?"

"Dinner is served, Herr President, at eight o'clock. The Grand Duke preferred it at that hour, which gave him plenty of time to dress."

The President was painfully startled. "Good God, did the man stay in bed all day long?"

Romsteck preserved an offended silence, which continued until Nyla came to the rescue.

"My father is accustomed to having onion soup for dinner. He counts on it very much. I suppose the chef—the chef would not mind, occasionally that is, preparing it for him?"

The butler seemed very much shocked.

"Onion soup, Fraulein?—Did I understand you to say onion soup?"

"Yes," said Guadeloupe. "You know, with toast in it, and plenty of cheese."

"Why, Herr President, I do not believe an onion has been served in the palace since the Reign of Terror."

Romsteck rang for the chef.

"Monsieur Pigalle," he said, "will you rehearse for the Herr President what dishes have been arranged for dinner this evening?"

Pigalle, with a Frenchman's eye for a pretty girl, was in his element.

"With the greatest pleasure. To welcome the President and his daughter I have planned as follows. The menu is plain, in deference to a republican simplicity of taste, but I hope not displeasing. *Hors d'œuvres variés*, served in the Adriatic fashion. To follow, *Homard Paprika*. I thought that then a *culotte de bœuf garnie, au vin de Madére;* or if that seems a trifle rich we could substitute *filets mignons piqués de truffes*. Not to overload the stomach, Mademoiselle, I thought that some pancakes burning in raspberry brandy would be amusing; followed by a *soufflé*, an ice, and some fruit. I feel sure that the Herr President and Mademoiselle will have no cause for complaint."

Herr Guadeloupe, to whom French was not only unfamiliar but an uncongenial tongue for political reasons, had no very clear idea of just what these phrases represented in the way of actual victuals.

" Any soup? " he asked.

" If desired, I can add a nice *julienne aux pointes d'asperges*," said Pigalle. " But I believe if the Herr President always knows in advance just what dishes are to be served, he deprives himself of much of the artistry of the table."

"I don't want artistry of the table, I just want some onion soup," thought the President, but refrained from saying it. With an air of dignity that seemed to make further discussion impossible, Romsteck and the chef withdrew.

" Well, I don't know any more than I did before," said Guadeloupe. " I told you this was going to be terrible." He began hunting about the room.

" Marvellous old furniture," said Nyla.

" I'm not looking at the furniture. I'm hunting for a box of matches. I think I'll go out in the garden and have a smoke."

A stir in the hall caught Nyla's attention.

" Oh, look, Daddy, our things have come." Through the tall glass doors she could see a troop of servants lined up respectfully to receive their very modest and shabby luggage, the portmanteaux and the battered tin trunk. She caught a glimpse of a familiar old brown satchel.

" I wish we had bought some new bags, it looks too absurd to see them all making such to-do over our poor old things. Your old satchel looks too awful."

" My satchel? " he said. " Is it there? Just what I need. There's a——"

" Now, Daddy, what are you going to do? You mustn't——"

But he sped into the hall where he surprised the assembled flunkeys by seizing the bag. Muttering some unintelligible explanation, he rushed into the salon with it. Two agitated footmen attempted to help, but he clung to the thing with feverish earnestness, opened it, rummaged among some socks and collars, and finally produced a packet of tobacco, a box of matches, and a bottle of brandy.

" There," he said. " By heaven, I've earned it."

He uncorked the bottle and sniffed it affectionately. With difficulty Nyla restrained him until one of the footmen had brought a tray and glasses. " Well," he said, pouring some out, " now we can feel a little more at home."

" Your pardon, Herr President," objected Romsteck who had suddenly appeared, " but those are not brandy glasses. They are champagne goblets."

" Major," retorted the harassed man, " I drink to your Grand Duke. I am beginning to understand why he fled." And he raised his glass. But before he could place it to his lips he was halted by a cry, courteous but peremptory.

"Just a moment, Herr President!" exclaimed a young man, striding into the room. "It is my duty." He took the glass from the hand of the astonished President and drank off the contents himself.

V

THE unannounced visitor was a man of about thirty, tall and sinewy, with curly auburn hair and jocular blue eyes. He was smartly dressed in excellently fitted brown tweeds. There was something engagingly droll in his brisk assurance and the sharp contour of his clean-shaven face. He stood holding the empty glass and pursed his lips with the thoughtful air of one critically considering some mooted nicety of degustation. Then he nodded approvingly and his severity relaxed. He smiled, bowed to Guadeloupe and Nyla, and brought forward a chair with practised grace.

" Be seated, Fraülein, I implore you," he said. " Young women have to be on their feet so much after they are married, I always urge them to take their ease while they can."

Nyla had a strong inclination to laugh, but conquered it. Romsteck, not less startled than the others, began to speak, but the stranger held up his hand with a commanding gesture.

"A thousand and one apologies, Herr President, for this lack of ceremony. Permit me." He took the bottle, chose a fresh glass, filled it and offered it with a charming obeisance. " I should, of course, have been here before your arrival. You were earlier than I expected."

Guadeloupe had a sagacious instinct of silence in perplexing situations. He contented himself by tossing off the postponed dram.

" My name is Cointreau, from the Department of Public Safety. My credentials."

He took a card from his pocket.

" I am authorized to ask a few moments' private interview with you—and with the Fraülein, of course. Butler, remove this debris and the Herr President and I can talk without interruption."

Romsteck, to his own surprise, found himself helping the footmen to clear away tea. He had not been spoken to in that voice of calm authority since the Grand Duke flitted.

" Heavenly old place, isn't it ? " said Cointreau to Nyla, in the casual tone of an old friend. " I hope you are going to be very happy here. I shall make it my business to see that you are. What a pretty frock. The printed chiffons are delightful, especially on the slender figures. Have a gasper ? "

" Why—thank you," said Nyla. " I'd love one, but I didn't know whether—in the palace——"

" Bosh! " cried the surprising young man. " Palaces are made to do what you like in."

32

With skilful legerdemain he snapped a match into flame on his thumbnail, a trick new to her, and gave her a light.

" You have no objection to a pipe? " he asked, taking out a well-glossed briar. " Isn't that a beauty? " he said, holding it out to the President. Guadeloupe, with the habit of the seasoned smoker, took it, sniffed the fragrant char in the bowl, and then produced his own.

" Now to business," proceeded the visitor. " Herr President, you'll forgive my abrupt entrance when I explain. The Department of Public Safety realizes that hitherto insufficient precautions have been taken to safeguard the persons of high officials. Particularly at the present time, in this new phase of our political life, it is essential that no accident of any sort should mar the success of the Illyrian Republic. You know what unfortunate repercussion it would have among the Great Powers if any unpleasantness arose in our affairs. I am acting as a special agent for the Department of Public Safety, but I may as well add, entirely in confidence, that I have authority from certain people in Geneva—I feel sure I need not be uncomfortably explicit."

Geneva never had to be mentioned more than once to secure Herr Guadeloupe's anxious attention.

Cointreau resumed his winning gaiety of manner.

33   D

"Please do not feel under any constraint, Herr President. My affair is to see that you— and Fräulein Nyla also—are completely comfortable and at home, free to give all your attention to those political problems that confront our country. You are aware that there are those—I need not specify—who would be happy to see the new republic embarrassed. You must have perfect confidence. Consider me, if you wish, not as a mere Secret Service officer, but as a kind of social secretary."

"Why, Daddy," cried Nyla. "How wonderful! Just what you wanted!"

"An imperfect instrument, Fräulein," said the special agent modestly, "but at your service. I need hardly say, Herr President, that for the success of my mission it must be entirely confidential. Nothing further need be said than that I am here on private business from the League. For your own sake, and to guard against any possible emergencies, it will be advisable to institute certain unobtrusive inspections of minor routine. We cannot afford to run any risks. It was for that reason that—too unceremoniously, I fear—I felt it wise to make certain of the brandy. It was excellent," he added.

"It was my own," said Guadeloupe. "But indeed, dear sir, you lift an anxiety from my mind. This is a difficult position in which I find myself, and a little intimate assistance, properly authorized of course——"

"Be quite at your ease!" exclaimed the special agent. "The last thing Ramsay Macdonald said to me at Geneva—you know Mac, I dare say; charming fellow—was, Do everything you can for Guadeloupe. It's very important he should make a go of it in Illyria, he and his lovely daughter."

Herr Guadeloupe, who had had hitherto much sterner monitions from the high contracting parties of Europe, was greatly pleased.

"That's very encouraging," he said. "Come, Herr Cointreau, since you approve the brandy, drink to the success of our young Republic."

They pledged it standing, with due formality.

"Herr President," said Cointreau, "if we play our cards carefully, you shall go down in history as the man who put Illyria on the map."

"Oh, I know he will," cried Nyla, enchanted. "Daddy's wonderful, Herr Cointreau, and if only that awful American debt can be paid——"

"Don't you worry a bit about the debt. That'll work out all right. Perhaps I can help a bit there: I visited in America once, I know how to handle them. Now the first thing is to make sure that all the more intimate matters are comfortable. Everything quite O.K.?"

35

There was something infectiously reassuring in the special agent's clear jovial gaze, and Herr Guadeloupe, blowing a cloud of comforting tobacco smoke, began to feel that there might be some fun in being President after all.

" Well," he said cautiously, " do you suppose there would be unfortunate repercussions at Geneva if I did not dress for dinner every evening? As you know, I am a plain man, Herr Cointreau, and too much formality——"

" Quite right, quite right," said Cointreau. " When Herriot was premier in France the same problem arose. You remember what excellent political capital he made of his pipe and his shirtsleeves. Geneva will understand perfectly. In fact, Herr President, I was about to say, I think that if anything your present outfit is even a little unnecessarily conventional. Also, I was observing your trousers—perhaps you would do me the favour of standing a moment."

The President rose, and Cointreau diligently examined the garments in various perspectives.

" They have their virtues, I can quite see," he said judicially. " The cut is eminently republican. No one, I think, would suspect you of royalist ambitions so long as you wear them. Allow me, without being too intimate—

the seat may be said to be roomy, meritorious in a sedentary garment."

Nyla broke into a delightful gust of laughter.

" Daddy thought that by tightening his suspenders a bit he could buck them up. Let's have a try."

" I'm afraid it's hopeless," said Cointreau. " No, we'll tackle the stabilization of the florin first. That presents fewer complexities. For the Herr President I suggest perfect informality—knickerbockers or whatever you please. You must not agitate yourself about niceties of deportment. I'll take care of all that. Fräulein Nyla, I think, should dress for dinner, because youth and beauty are so well set off by *décolleté*."

" I had not supposed," said the President, " that the League would be so attentive to detail."

" What the League desires is gaiety. After these painful years a little guileless merriment will be the best possible tonic for business. The last thing Ramsay Macdonald said to me was, ' Tell them to be sprightly. It will reassure the foreign investors who are going to buy the Illyrian bonds.' "

" That must have been the next-to-the-last thing he said," observed Nyla.

" They have said so many things at Geneva, possibly I get the exact order confused.—I think you remarked, Herr President, that that was your own brandy? In that case it would be wise, before we go any further, to be sure that the refreshment provided by the State is equally correct. You will understand that in the work of the Department we cannot afford to neglect any possibilities, however trifling. —Is there a bell? Oh, no matter——"

He tapped vigorously with his pipestem against his empty glass.

" If you will kindly explain to your butler, we can make a beginning in our necessary inspections."

" This is Herr Cointreau, from Geneva," said Guadeloupe when Romsteck had been summoned. " He is here on diplomatic business of a private nature."

" I shall have to make a few precautionary examinations of the household routine," said Cointreau. " We will begin by interviewing the cellar-man. Send him in, and tell him to bring his inventory."

VI

THE special agent, after careful study of Karl's lists, thought that the 1865 cognac should be tested first. It proved to be of the finest possible bouquet, gentle, mellow, and volatile.

" I am greatly relieved," he said graciously. " To tell the truth, I had feared that during the confusions of reconstruction things might have been allowed to run down. I express my personal satisfaction that the wine-steward is worthy of Farniente traditions." He dismissed Karl, who departed beaming.

" It is unfortunate," he added, " that there does not seem to be a cocktail shaker anywhere in the palace. I shall have to give the butler a lesson in the mixing of cocktails. I know, from experience in Paris and Geneva, how useful they are in coming to an understanding with American diplomats. However, we can go into these matters more fully by and by."

The President had by this time recovered some of his naturally sanguine spirits. He mentioned the onion soup problem to his advisor, who promised to arrange everything.

"Herr President," he said, "you can repose the most perfect confidence in me. Imagine me a kind of Colonel House, taciturn, far-seeing and discreet. In fact you may call me Colonel, if you will. It adds to the dignity of the situation."

"My daughter and I shall be disappointed if you do not stay to dinner, Colonel."

"With pleasure. There is much to be attended to. To-morrow I will assure myself that the car is in proper order for your use and that the driver understands what routes are to be followed when you go through the city. The Department of Public Safety was often very anxious during the reign of the Grand Duke. He went about with such reckless freedom, drinking at cafés, meeting ladies for supper—you will not compel me to elaborate the theme. It would be undesirable for your chauffeur to drive across wide open spaces, where bullets—but let's not be alarmist. It is only that I am personally responsible to the Department."

"Nonsense!" cried Nyla, giving her father a hug. "No one would want to hurt my adorable Daddy."

"Alas, Fräulein, the payment of the war debts implies heavy taxation; and heavy taxation always means a certain amount of gunning for statesmen."

"There's rather a nasty place in the Red

Room," said Guadeloupe nervously. " A window where people used to hide and shoot at the Duke. You might have a look at it." He crossed to the mantel and studied the bullet holes in the panelling. He was relieved to see them well above the level of his head.

" These medieval houses are just full of hiding-places," remarked Cointreau.

Herr Guadeloupe excused himself to go and unpack his official papers. Nyla was a little uncertain whether she was in the position of the visitor's hostess or not, but his easy frankness made embarrassment impossible.

" Come," he suggested, " let's have a look round. What a stunning old place it is! This ballroom floor—perfect for dancing! We must have a little music presently. And the terrace—delightful place to cool off between dances. Something green, I was thinking——"

" Something green? " Nyla did not quite follow the quick transitions of the special agent's mind; but she understood, of course, that men accustomed to dispatch complicated international business would live at a speedier tempo than the simple libertads of a rustic republic.

" For your frock. Something green, of an airy floating nature, and the stockings that are so popular in Paris just now—the colour of Camembert cheese—would be the very thing for dancing. A few Chinese lanterns, not too many, strung here on the terrace. And, by Jove, how well a canoe would go on the moat."

Nyla was wondering, a little uncomfortably, whether her quite modest wardrobe was chic enough to satisfy the exacting tastes of this connoisseur of modes. She was a charming figure as she sat on the old stone balustrade that bounded the terrace. The still water beneath reflected the pointed towers of Farniente and the great chestnut trees in the park.

" I'm so sorry," she said. " I don't think I have anything in green. You are a most versatile person. Do you undertake the millinery details for all the new republics? "

Her touch of irony, if it was irony, did not at all abash Cointreau. His enthusiasm was irresistible.

" Few of the republics, Fräulein, have such reasons for enlisting one's co-operation."

" I had no idea the League was so far-reaching in its organization."

" We try to give Service. You see, we've learned a great deal from the American experts who come to Geneva. One of the things Illyria needs just now is Publicity. We'll get some good photographs into the American Sunday papers: first thing you know the tourists will be coming here in crowds. That'll be good for trade. You see, your father will be busy with parliamentary affairs, he can't

possibly think of all these other things. I want
to help him all I can.—And help you too,
Fräulein," he added. " Even in palaces young
women may get bored. Sometimes you may
feel like slipping away to the cinema. We can
go to see Douglas Fairbanks together."

Nyla was enchanted. The arrival of this
attractive, experienced and sophisticated gentleman, so eager to assume responsibilities,
seemed to puff away the secret anxieties she
had felt as to life at Farniente.

" I *do* want Daddy to be a successful President," she said with girlish earnestness. " It's
a terribly hard job. Of course his opponents
in parliament are frightfully jealous, they'd
do anything to spoil his record. He's so
wonderfully simple and honest, he only
thinks of the good of the country."

" Now don't you worry a bit," he reassured
her. " We're all going to have a gorgeous time.
You know that lawn in front of the house
would be just the place for some of the old
Illyrian folk dances. I dare say we could get
the chambermaids to put on their peasant
costume and hop about. It would be just the
thing to amuse any busybodies that float in
from the Great Powers. Take their minds off
the poor old florin."

A dim far-away pulsation had been softly
discernible in the summer air; now, from the
direction of the Pannonia Platz a burst of

43

shrill music was unmistakable. It came nearer and resolved itself into the anthem of the Illyrian Republic. A young radical poet had sat up all night, during the recent Revolution, to put new ejaculations to an old national air. As a republican hymn it was completely successful, one verse extolled Democracy, one Freedom, and one the Proletariat (a difficult word to find rhymes for). A parliamentary committee had expunged the stanza levelled against foreign capital, which was considered tactless under the circumstances; otherwise the lyric had gone through with acclaim, and was now being sung on all possible occasions.

" Oh," exclaimed Nyla, " it must be the Demonstration. Daddy thought he'd escaped it by coming early, but they've followed him here. His supporters, and the interviewers from the Labour papers. He was hoping they wouldn't come until he'd got a little bit settled. If those people from the *New Freedom* and the *Folkvoice* find him surrounded by uniformed flunkeys I'm sure it'll be bad for politics."

" Quick! " cried Cointreau, his eyes bright with excitement. " This is important. Hurry upstairs, tell your father to put on his old clothes. Get that housekeeper person, what's her name, Innsbruck, to call the maids together and have them wear their native duds. I'll tell Romsteck to roll out a barrel of beer

44

on the lawn. I'll keep the crowd amused at the front steps until your father's ready. Tell him to bring his pipe. Hurry!"

With a flutter of skirts Nyla fled across the terrace.

Herr Romsteck, already sufficiently agitated by the events of the day, was in the hall wondering if the parade now advancing down the avenue of limes presaged another *coup d'état*. In the days of the Grand Duke gatherings of the rabble never approached nearer than the tall iron grille on the Pannonia Platz. The music sounded louder and louder, green and white flags fluttered above the throng. He looked anxiously at the cheerful envoy from Geneva, who strolled in from the salon, smiling genially. Romsteck could not account for the presence of this unexplained visitor, but he recognized the manners of one accustomed to command.

" Romsteck," said Cointreau, " this is a jocund moment."

" Jocund, sir? It looks like another revolution."

" A great proletarian celebration. The innocent high spirits for which Illyria was famous in the old days. Do you dance? "

" Dance? " ejaculated the major-domo, horrified at such flippancy. " Not in public, sir; far from it, sir."

" But you shall," said Cointreau firmly.

45

" We shall all dance. It is important to impress the populace with our democratic simplicity. Geneva and the Great Powers expect it of us. For the sake of European concord, old son, you must lay aside that priestly dignity. We will have folk-dancing on the lawn, and you and Frau Innsbruck shall lead the revels."

Romsteck's orderly little world seemed to be turning topsy-turvy. He gazed inhospitably at the plebeian crowd already pressing into the sacred courtyard. They marched orderly and with respectful mien, an honest bourgeois procession, but now the band broke out again and the windows quivered.

" Get busy," ordered Cointreau. " Hop to it, or you lose your job. Have the cellar-man broach a cask of beer by the front steps. Tell the footmen to take off their coats and appear in breeches, with coloured kerchiefs. Come and tell me when the President's ready, before he shows himself, so I can introduce him properly."

Cointreau's first words, as he stood on the front steps and gestured for silence, were a masterpiece of demagogic skill.

" Citizens," he said, " the President of the Republic——"

Cheers.

" Will greet you himself——"

Loud Cheers.

46

" As soon as he has finished his onion soup."

Terrific enthusiasm. The crowd enjoyed the allusion, flags waved, the bass drum was pounded, men shouted, woman huzzaed, children squeaked.

" It would not be like Herr Guadeloupe to alter the established simplicity of his life because his fellow-citizens have put him here at Farniente to represent the Republic. He asks me to tell you that he wants this little celebration to be in the true Illyrian style. There will be cookies for the young, beer for the thirsty, and our old Illyrian folk-dances on the lawn."

In all its long history Farniente had never witnessed a more cordial scene. Slopes of westering sunshine poured across the mossy roof of the palace, gilding the increasing crowd that came curiously hurrying down the avenue. Dogs barked and frolicked on the outskirts. Sentries laid down their arms and fraternized with the mob. Romsteck, in the worried conviction that all this meant insurrection unless the throng was pacified, hurried out the beer and produced baskets of pretzels and cakes from his secret stores. The Illyrian instinct for popular merrymaking, long repressed during days of disastrous war and political uncertainty, now blossomed in bright flower.

Cointreau kept the crowd together by a few cheerful and patriotic remarks until, just at the psychological moment, Herr Guadeloupe appeared, wearing a knickerbocker suit and puffing his pipe. The people shouted applause. Cointreau, taking a mouth-organ from his pocket, led the band in another explosion of the national hymn. Guadeloupe, flushed with emotion, made a brief speech which was exactly the right sort of thing. His old knickerbockers and the pipe warm in his hand lent him that ease of mind so necessary to the political orator. By the time he had finished, each of his hearers felt that it was by personal favour of the Deity that he had been born an Illyrian. The cheers were deafening and the barrel of beer was unbunged. The corps of maids, charming in short green kilts and red jackets, bare knees and white stockings, filed demurely from the service wing. The special agent, still playing the mouth-organ, seized Nyla as his partner and led off a foursome country dance with Romsteck and Frau Innsbruck. These worthies perspired with embarrassment and began the measure with stiff clumsiness, but Cointreau's mouth-organ and his comic zeal warmed them somewhat. The spectators, at first respectfully puzzled, gradually began to applaud. Then Innsbruck, slipping on a juicy bit of turf, fell rump-flat. The populace yelled and the ice was broken.

48

Chambermaids, footmen, and the citizens themselves, joined in. A dozen different groups of dancers were formed, the band struck up peasant airs and yodels familiar to all, and the President himself, seizing a stout matron, capered with gusto.

Colonel Cointreau circulated helpfully in the gay rout. The humorous cantata of his mouth-organ was heard wherever the mirth was thickest. Evidently his severe life as an international negotiator had not dimmed a simple human relish for comely females; he was seen footing an intricate morris with Lorli, Nyla's pretty tire-woman; he lined up the chambermaids to be photographed, amid much laughter and broad jest, himself slipping modestly away whenever a lens was pointed in his direction. When in the unusual exertion Frau Innsbruck burst some private reef-points and ruptured a garter, the Colonel was first to seize the tensile fragment and hail it as a tender trophy. It was so long since Frau Innsbruck's garter had had any publicity or been the object of competition or sartorial strain that the housekeeper went moist and ruddy with pleased confusion.

" It's easy to see he's a real aristocrat," she confided to Romsteck as they withdrew from active participation. " He's as lively as the Grand Duke. I wish *he* were President." She had a vague feeling that with so sportive a

E

person around there might, even in a Republic, be some chance for the winsome intrigue that makes life tolerable to females. Even the scandalized Romsteck, gazing where Geneva's expert was now astride the beer-keg, hastening the flow by mouth-organ madrigals, had to admit that the Colonel had done much to enliven the party.

The President also was not far from the beer, cheerfully engrossed in talk with the reporters, who wore the specially professional look of those who approve what they have seen and are getting ready to write a favourable story for the papers. Nyla, seeing her father's air of satisfaction, was thoroughly happy. The Colonel insisted on dancing repeatedly; in these country measures he was agile rather than practised, but there was a pleasant quaintness in his figures and he had a piquant habit of uttering enigmatic phrases.

" Never go in for politics without a mouth-organ and a pair of rubber heels," was one of these.

" Rubber heels? " she inquired, the next time the pattern of the dance brought them together for a few moments.

" An American invention," he replied. " Very useful for statesmen."

Presently they retired to a corner of the lawn overlooking the water. From a distance they watched the crowd now beginning to disperse, Herr Guadeloupe gaily shaking hands, the enthusiastic citizens breaking out into little ripples of cheering.

" I don't know how to thank you, Colonel."

" *You* don't need to call me Colonel," he replied. " I just suggested that for your father."

" What shall I call you, then? "

" Let's wait and see. Something may suggest itself. You can begin with Gene, if you like. Short for Geneva."

" You've given Daddy a wonderful send-off," she said. " I don't know what he'll do when you go back to the League."

" Oh, I shan't go back. They expect me to stay here and keep an eye on things.—On people, too," he added, looking at her with cheerful admiration. " I have quite an eye for the picturesque."

" Are you really an Illyrian? " she asked. " You're so different. Your accent——"

" I've been a great deal abroad."

There was a brief silence.

" You know," he said, " I had intended simply to make a daily inspection, to make sure that everything was O.K. But I can see that the situation is unusual. I believe it would be wiser to take up quarters right here in the palace. Then I should be on hand in case— well, in case I could be useful. Suppose you fell into the moat, for instance. The Department of Public Safety has to guard against all sorts of possibilities."

" But I can swim. Besides, I don't believe it's deep."

" We'll go out one of these days and see. There's an old punt down there that'd do for a canoe."

He vaulted lightly to a seat on the licheny old bastion and played a gay little strain on his mouth-organ.

" We might compose a moating song," he reflected. " Something like this."

He improvized a few insinuating bars.

" A new kind of sea chanty, the moating song. Sentimental ditty: *If you and I were moating, Beneath the old chateau——*" He paused, hunting a rhyme. " Let's see, boat-ing, coating, doting——"

" *And idling there and floating,*" she suggested.

" Good girl! Say, you're a poet. *And idling there and floating In our petit bateau——*"

" *We'd drift about, not noting——*"

" *The taxes and the voting——*"

" *For pleasures beyond quoting——*"

" *Just you and I would know,*" he finished with delight. " Great stuff! We could write a new anthem for the Republic that'd beat that other one all hollow. Now let's get the music right."

" You said I ought to dress for dinner. I'd

better go and see if I've got anything to wear that you'd approve of. And if you're going to stay, how about your luggage?"

"Bless you," he said calmly, "it's here. I brought it with me. Tell old Rumpsteak to pick me out a nice room without any eastern windows. I hate to be waked up by the sun in my eyes."

The small wheedle of the mouth-organ sounded gaily behind her as she walked across the lawn. The Colonel was perfecting his Moating Song.

VII

NYLA, whose acquaintance with men was limited, had never seen so unusual and charming a person. Colonel Cointreau's immaculate evening dress and his gay affable talk eased the embarrassments of the elaborate dinner-table; even Herr Guadeloupe forgot to miss the onion soup for one evening. The Colonel complimented Nyla on her frock, patted her arm encouragingly as he escorted her to the dining-room, and tutored the President in the choice of forks and spoons with such unobtrusive grace that no one could have been offended. Indeed in another land one would have said that the Colonel had been raised from boyhood on the Book of Etiquette and Twenty Minutes a Day with the Harvard Classics. He restrained the President from tucking his napkin into his collar, deftly removed the bread-crust when Guadeloupe began using it to sponge up the last of a rich gravy, and his gentle " I think the other spoon, Herr President " was like a parenthetical refrain in his fluent conversation. Illyrian table manners, as travellers have noted, are often a form of rapid transit rather than a social ceremony, but the Colonel was very patient. " You must remember the effect on our American bondholders," was his persuasive reminder when the President seemed a little restless under discipline.

After dinner Herr Guadeloupe was allowed to compose himself with his favourite game of patience, and three aces in the first row of cards helped to solace him. The Colonel, sitting with Nyla by candle-light on an old brocade sofa, remarked that the romantic and sentimental associations of Farniente were stimulating to anyone sensitive to such influences.

" History keeps repeating itself," he said, alluding to the gallant career of the Grand Duke.

" I don't suppose that matters," said Nyla, " as long as it repeats pleasant things."

Somehow they had embarked upon palmistry, which the Colonel said was often a valuable aid to statesmanship.

" This is so much pleasanter than the League headquarters at Geneva," he averred. " A dull place, full of card indexes and diplomatic dossiers. Now your hand, Fräulein, is obviously that of a loyal, frank, and affectionate nature, full of generous impulses that should be encouraged. What a pity I could not have studied it long ago. I could have told that you were destined for high things. See

55

how the life-line slants upward. I see a long life. There are at least sixty happy years before you, full of interest."

" Just about long enough to pay off the American debt," said the President. " You don't see anything there about a rate of interest higher than one per cent, do you? Because if so, we're done for."

" I see surprises caused by strangers from abroad," said the Colonel, examining closely and tenderly. He was about to remark how beautiful the terrace would be in the moonlight when Romsteck brought in a telegram.

" Gott! " cried Guadeloupe as he read the message. " You're right. He's coming at once."

" Who? " exclaimed the palmist.

" The American. And not just a commissioner, a full-fledged ambassador. That means we'll have to put him up here, as a matter of courtesy, until he finds a house. Lord, I didn't suppose he'd come until we'd got straightened out. How can I explain that the new taxation isn't in effect yet?"

" You'll have to keep his mind off financial matters until things are settled," said the Colonel. " We'll give him a big dinner and a ball. We'll take him moating. We'll sing him our moating song."

" Do you speak American? " asked Nyla. " Daddy and I know very little."

" Enough to get along with."

" Well, you'll have to interpret for me,"
said the worried President. " Good God, I
must speak to the Finance Minister at once,"
and he fled to Farniente's one telephone.

Even the imperturbable Cointreau seemed
a little troubled as he read the telegram that
still lay on the card table. It said :—

> *Congratulations your inauguration united
> states congress voted full recognition illyrian
> republic hon ulysses quackenbush now in
> geneva accompanied frau quackenbush will
> proceed farniente discuss debt settlement
> quackenbush very influential united states
> probably eventual ambassador very important
> show all possible courtesies secretariat league
> of nations.*

" Worse and worse," said the President,
returning a few minutes later. " He's coming
to-morrow."

VIII

THE Cabinet, hastily summoned, met
next morning in the Red Room with
many controversial topics to discuss. As Herr
Guadeloupe had feared, one of the puny gilt
chairs proved unequal to the anxious shiftings
of Herr Leutz, the obese Finance Minister.
But even under Romsteck's censorious eye a
broken chair was the least of the President's
anxieties. Herr Leutz stayed to lunch, to discuss further details of the fiscal statements to
be laid before the American ambassador, but
Colonel Cointreau and Nyla were nowhere
to be seen. The absence of his privy councillor
when events of such delicacy were toward,
agitated Herr Guadeloupe.

The Colonel had risen that morning in the
highest spirits and began his inspections with
vigour. The President, who slept but ill that
first night in such unaccustomed quarters,
had not finished shaving when he had heard
cheery whistling outdoors, and observed the
Genevan sculling round the moat in the old
punt. The special agent appeared at the
breakfast board with a somewhat miscellaneous bundle of flowers and cresses that he

58

had picked on the grassy foreshore of the stream. These posies, apologizing for their Ophelia-like aspect, he presented to Nyla. After breakfast he made a careful tour of the house with Frau Innsbruck, inquiring into everything with the liveliest interest and humour. In the kitchen he ingratiated himself with Pigalle and made suggestions as to the menu in honour of Herr Quackenbush. Upstairs he praised the linen closets, complimented the housemaids on their thoroughness in airing the beds, and somewhat startled Nyla by the experienced domesticity of his comments. He wanted to be assured that she had enough hangers for her gowns and that her dressing-table mirror was in a good light. Then, suddenly admiring the clarity and brilliance of the weather, he insisted that now was the time to make sure that the Presidential car was in good running order. He satisfied himself that the tank was filled with essence and dismissed the chauffeur. He and Nyla rolled gaily away down the avenue in the elderly but impressive limousine, on which the shield of Illyria was freshly enamelled over the erased coronet of the Grand Duke.

They had not returned by the time lunch was over, and the President was annoyed. Herr Leutz, moreover, had been a depressing companion. Like all conscientious treasurers of an insolvent exchequer he had a hundred

irrefutable reasons for the red ink in his
ledgers: his remarks about the dangerous
flatulence of the Illyrian currency were only
too true. He obviously disapproved the luxury
of the President's surroundings, and seemed
with sombre eye to be mentally converting
the Grand Ducal plate into new florins.
Guadeloupe, sharpened by Colonel Cointreau into observation of such matters, noted
that the Finance Minister was an untidy eater
and resolved that he must not be placed too
near Frau Quackenbush at the state dinner.
"They *might* have given me," he reflected bitterly, "at least one Cabinet member who
could be trusted to make a pleasing impression
on our foreign creditors."

As he escorted Herr Leutz to the door,
Guadeloupe was thinking secretly of a nap.
He was weary, and would need all possible
freshness for the evening. Romsteck was not
visible, and the President had a mental picture of stealing upstairs, removing his boots,
and stretching out for a recuperative hour.
But at that moment Lorli appeared, and curt-
sied charmingly.

"I'm sorry, Herr President, but it's time
for you and the Herr Minister to take the
dancing lesson."

"Dancing lesson?" ejaculated the President. "What on earth do you mean?"

"Colonel Cointreau left positive orders

that after lunch you and Herr Leutz were to practise in the ballroom."

" Impossible," said Herr Leutz, making for the door. " I have sixteen different deficits to analyse."

" Colonel Cointreau said, Herr President, that interests of state absolutely required that both you and Herr Leutz should dance with Frau Quackenbush this evening."

" Old Pannonian deities!" exclaimed Guadeloupe. " What human being can practise dancing immediately after lunch? " But there was a look of such certainty in Lorli's pretty face that he felt himself crumbling. He laid hold of Leutz's coat-tails.

" Here," he said sharply, " if I've got to go through with this, you must too."

" The Colonel said the League would expect it," announced Lorli respectfully.

" Double damn the Colonel," complained the resentful President. " Why isn't he here himself to help me? He said that was what he came for. Now he's off somewhere with Nyla in the only decent car. Leutz, if he doesn't get back in time *you'll* have to meet Herr Quackenbush at the station, in the flivver. At any rate that will impress him with the state of our finances."

They followed Lorli like two guilty schoolboys. In the ballroom they found a determined-looking trio: Pigalle to play the piano,

Frau Innsbruck to represent the Quackenbush, Romsteck to supervize. The major-domo
had already removed all small gilded chairs
from Herr Leutz's access.

"Dancing of the ballroom sort," he said
solemnly to his two pupils, "is very different
from the rustic manœuvres we executed yesterday. Owing to the greater intimacy of
personal contact, all the more grace of deportment is necessary. It was the Grand Duke's
custom, in these affairs, always to begin by
inviting any lady he specially desired to
honour to accompany him in a lively fox-trot.
For example."

He bowed magnificently to Frau Innsbruck, motioned to Pigalle who struck up
some spirited and mischievous syncopations,
and swam off with the housekeeper into a
species of rotating pedestrianism with occasional sideways slidings. To the President,
who was totally unfamiliar with modern
dancing, it seemed completely absurd. Frau
Innsbruck's solid figure, moulded on the
Queen Victoria contour, floated with genteel
gravity in this antic demonstration.

"So," said Romsteck, bringing the lady to
port alongside the reluctant chief magistrate.
"Now the Herr President and the Herr
Minister are to imagine themselves entering
the ballroom with their partners. The music
begins, they are off."

Even in this emergency Herr Guadeloupe's presence of mind did not wholly
desert him. He felt that he would learn better
with Lorli, so he moved to grasp her, in-
tending to leave the housekeeper to the embrace of Herr Leutz. But Romsteck inter-
vened. " With Frau Innsbruck, if you please.
It will be better practice. She has the mature
configuration, such as we may assume Frau
Quackenbush to possess."

The music seemed terribly rapid to the
two pupils as they struggled to imitate what
they had seen. " *One*, two, three and four
and *one*, two, three and four and," counted
Romsteck, pursuing them with advice. " The
Herr President will control his impulse to leap
and caper. Feet flat on the floor. A gliding
walk, hollow back, stiff in the hips. If desired,
just the least rearward oscillation of the pelvic
region, to suggest enthusiasm. Not to excess,
however, Herr President, that would not be
expected."

Innsbruck, thrilled in spite of herself by
the honour of dancing with the President,
tried hard to help him. He struggled nobly,
with his eyes on his feet, but when he happened to catch sight of Herr Leutz's large
boots shuffling miserably among Lorli's twink-
ling members the spectacle unnerved him.
He lost count, faltered and came to a stop.

" It's too difficult," he said hopelessly.

" Better for the debt settlement if I don't attempt it. I'll get Colonel Cointreau to do it for me."

" Once again, Herr President, by yourself, to get the rhythm," insisted the major-domo, and Guadeloupe performed a lugubrious *pas seul*.

" The Herr President's trousers handicap him," commented Romsteck, walking beside him in his course and studying his morbid gyrations.

" Well I'm not going to dance without them, even for Frau Quackenbush," he retorted.

" That was not my suggestion," said Romsteck disapprovingly. " I mean that they impede by reason of their longitude. If the Herr President will permit——" He rolled up several inches of the drooping tubes, and sent for some of the 1865 cognac to hearten the sufferers.

With this refreshment things went a little better. Taking advantage of a pause by Herr Leutz to mop his broad brow, the President cut in on Lorli; he found her more stimulating as a partner. Both pupils were busily treading the measure when a cheerful hail surprised them. Cointreau and Nyla entered, radiant with health and enjoyment.

" Bravo, bravo! " cried the Colonel. " Herr President, you are the soul of legerity. And the Finance Minister, treading with a toe of swan's down, like a man walking on red-hot budgets."

"Your merriment is ill-timed, Colonel," said Guadeloupe peevishly. " I thought you came to Farniente to help me, and here you have been absent for hours when I needed you."

"You mustn't be angry, Daddy," said Nyla, looking so sunburned and pretty that no one could have been. " We got lost in the hills. The Colonel was trying to find some goldenrod, it's a favourite American flower, and he thought it would be a delicate compliment to Frau Quackenbush."

" Certainly more delicate than my dancing with her would be," said the President.

"A good thing we *did* go," remarked Cointreau. " The car was in terrific condition. The valves need grinding, the clutch is dicky, the steering-wheel's loose, and she's simply crusty with carbon. We got the goldenrod though, a whole taxi full."

" Taxi full? " asked Guadeloupe.

" Yes," Nyla explained. " You see, the car went bad at Laibach and we had to hire a cab to come home."

" From Laibach? " exclaimed the Finance Minister. " It's fifty kilometres! "

" It's quite all right, Herr Treasurer," said Cointreau hastily. " I arranged to have him send the bill to Geneva. Come then, to our affair. Music, please! "

Pigalle rippled the keys, and while the two unpromising pupils slithered heavily at their task the Colonel and Nyla hovered blithely about them, twirling humorous patterns round the small area in which the others plodded conscientiously. The pair swooped and skimmed like gulls around a group of wounded porpoises, and the indignant President, amazed at his daughter's grace, paused to watch. They danced almost as though they had been professional partners, and Cointreau, maliciously pretending himself to be Guadeloupe, called out suggestions as he and Nyla coasted to and fro. These suggestions he illustrated with appropriate action.

" Observe, Herr President, you are now dancing with Frau Quackenbush. A few perfectly simple rhythms to begin with, until Frau Quackenbush begins to enter into the spirit of the occasion.—American women are cold, and require wooing.—Then, as she begins to respond, your confidence increases.—You murmur agreeable impromptus, complimentary and insinuating, into her ear—which will not be far away.—This is your first visit to Illyria, Frau Quackenbush? We must make it memorable.—Then, venturing upon more complex figures.—Now, perhaps, when she melts a little you steer toward a quiet corner.

—Surely, Frau Quackenbush, a great opulent country like yours will not be too hard on us in the matter of the debt? You will say a word in our behalf to the Ambassador? "

They came to a halt, Nyla rather flushed by the ardour the Colonel had put into his demonstration. Guadeloupe was just a little scandalized, and for a moment was the parent rather than the President.

" Here," he said sharply, " where did you learn to dance like that? "

" We practised a bit in the hotel at Laibach," she said. " While we were waiting for lunch."

Cointreau, enthusiastic as ever, was for having all the chambermaids summoned, to provide a realistic rehearsal of the evening ceremony. He also was eager that the President and Frau Innsbruck should attempt a Charleston together. But Guadeloupe had had enough.

" If Frau Quackenbush is to be melted, I leave it to you," he said.

" I should prefer to remain in the background. The League does not like its representatives to push themselves forward," said the Colonel with unexpected modesty. " Besides, I have a headache. I believe I overexerted myself testing the car. I was thinking of remaining in my room this evening."

" Heavens, no! " cried the President,

aghast. " My dear Colonel, I can't get on without you. I absolutely count on you as my interpreter."

" If I appear," said Cointreau, " I think it should be in uniform. A man looks much better dancing in some regalia."

" The Grand Duke left a whole wardrobe of uniforms," said Romsteck.

" Anything with a good splash of colour in it ? "

" The dress uniform as honorary admiral in the Dalmatian Navy arrived just before the War. His Grace never had an opportunity to wear it."

" True," said the Colonel. " I remember that the Dalmatian Navy spent the War prudently in dry-dock. I should have preferred a uniform with a more glorious record. However —blue and gold, with a cocked hat, will do very well."

" Choose whatever you like," said the President. " But remember I rely on you. And you promised to teach me a few American phrases of courtesy, that I can use when I run short."

IX

EVIDENTLY relations between Nyla and the Colonel had ripened prosperously during their outing. The President having gone off for his much-needed nap, these two explored the old north tower, and on the dark stairway the Colonel's arm stole protectively round her. The famous Purple Room, so-called from its rich wine-coloured hangings, was lighted only by a narrow casement in the six-foot stone fortification; it was a funereal place with a stale flavour of ancient orgy. The painted dado, perhaps fortunately, was scarcely visible in the dim light. The Colonel struck a match, but after one glimpse of Paphian distempers he extinguished it hastily. Always sensitive to psychic influences, he seemed a little depressed, and spoke gloomily of the difficulties of his career as an agent of international amenity.

" The trouble with this League of Nations work is, it's so uncertain. Here to-day and gone to-morrow."

" Don't say that," replied Nyla gently. " Besides, this is to-day."

" Geneva is so capricious. Sometimes I'll

barely get started on a job when orders will come to buzz off somewhere else. You never know when some delicate situation will arise that needs expert attention. They push you round so suddenly, sometimes you don't even have time to say good-bye."

There was just room for two to lean side by side, rather close, in the wedge-shaped recess of the window, looking out across the quiet water to the groves of the park. Nyla sympathetically returned the pressure of his hand, and looked admiringly at his handsome clear-cut features, now clouded with melancholy. This was a new phase of the volatile Colonel. Evidently beneath his frolic humour there was a deeper side.

" One hardly has time to put down roots anywhere, really become attached to—to places or people—before he's moved on. And I have great capacities for putting down roots," he continued wistfully.

" But where there are roots there are flowers," said Nyla, hardly knowing what she said. This softness in a strong character moved her strangely.

" Not always. Sometimes just weeds, or poison ivy."

" But even if you had to go back to Geneva, that isn't so terribly far. The League would let you run up and spend a week-end with us now and then."

The Colonel shook his head hopelessly.

" They usually send me a long way off—Poland, Greece, Armenia where the massacres are. Even to North America."

" There must be some mistake. They wouldn't send you to places like that if they knew the sort of man you are," said Nyla adoringly. " Or perhaps they're jealous of you at headquarters. Probably some of the people there are afraid you'll get their jobs."

" Darling," replied the Colonel.

" It's surprising," he added presently, " how small-minded people can be. Some of those department heads at Geneva would deny my very existence if it suited them to do so. That's what bureaucracy leads to. But whatever happens, you must always think tenderly of—of the League," he said generously. " It is a very noble and complicated organization."

Poor Nyla was almost in tears.

" Gene, don't talk like that about—the League. You *have* put down roots; I can feel them growing."

The Colonel was not anxious to linger unduly in the Purple Room, lest the Grand Duke's murals became too visible.

" Let's see if we can find that secret passage," he suggested when she was a little comforted.

The door to the cellar of the tower was

locked, but only with a padlock on a rusty hasp.

" No need to bother Romsteck," he said. " He might not like our snooping about." He fetched a poker from the fireplace in the Purple Room and easily snapped the fixture.

The cellar, at the foot of a winding stair, had probably once been a guard-room or storage place. The Colonel was amused to find carefully laid away several dozen of the old Burgundies which, according to Karl's manifests, had been exhausted by visiting plenipotentiaries.

" Ha!" he said. "This entry can be regarded as legitimate inspection. I suppose I really should report it to the League; sequestration of supplies, contrary to the Treaty. However, we'll be lenient. You see, alas, why international agents grow cynical."

The safety valve, as the Grand Duke always called his secret passage, was so cunningly concealed that a less ingenious investigator might have missed it. They tapped and sounded the walls without success, but then the Colonel fell to studying the coat-of-arms, elaborately carved and painted, high over the huge fireplace. It was surmounted by a visored helmet.

" There's something queer about that visor," he said. Climbing on a chair he reached up to it with the poker. The piece worked on a hinge, he pushed it upward, and with a soft rumble the iron fireback in the hearth slid aside. Behind was a tunnelled opening.

" Fine stuff! " he cried triumphantly. " Forward, adventurers! Look out for your dress, Nyla, it's a bit sooty. Hang on to my coat-tail." He pulled out his mouth-organ and gave a lively rendition of the moating song.

The passage, solidly lined with stone, was pitch dark, moist and draughty, but there was an old candle on the mantelpiece which he managed to shield with his hands. They groped cautiously through with no more mishap than a few mudstains. Eventually they reached a flight of stone steps where a crack of brightness showed above. A little vigorous pushing and the Colonel burst through a trap-door. They were in a small summer-house, discreetly screened by rhododendrons. Two hundred feet away, beyond the moat, lifted the old silvery masonry of the north tower.

"Excellent!" he said, rubbing the earth from his palms. " A little grimy for ladies, I fear. Now we'll go back and cover up our traces."

Nyla was eager to tell her father of their discovery, but Cointreau suggested that the President already had too much on his mind. " Let's keep this our secret, for the moment," he said. " People who work for the League are always stuffed with secrets. Now I think I had better go and try on that uniform."

X

HERR GUADELOUPE, refreshed by a good snooze, descended in a more hopeful mood. As he entered the salon, however, he halted in alarm, fearing another of those scenes of violence for which the palace was famous. Silhouetted against the tall windows was a menacing figure, with arms raised above its head and holding an object of dangerous shape. A bomb, thought the President, and dodged hastily behind the high-backed sofa. But Romsteck, standing by, seemed calm even if disapproving. Looking again, the President saw that it was Cointreau, glittering in blue and gold, with a sword in a scarlet sash and a cocked hat with a plume. Apparently he was in a state of violent passion: his arms were lifted and quivering as if in imprecation; he was agitating a vase wrapped in a napkin, from which came a rattling sound.

"What ho!" said the Colonel. "How do you like the Dalmatian Admiral? Pretty nifty. I'm giving the Major his first lesson in cocktails. I got the shaker from the hotel at Laubach. They'll send the bill for it to old Leutz. I thought the Republic ought to own one."

He continued to brandish while the others watched in doubtful silence; then he poured three doses of pale yellowish fluid and held out two of them.

" Try that, boys," he said familiarly. " Where I come from that's supposed to be the River of Lethe at high tide."

" In Geneva? " asked the President innocently.

" Geneva! " exclaimed the Colonel scornfully, but then checked himself. " Yes, exactly. Indeed, Herr President, the word *gin* is merely an abbreviation of Geneva, as any dictionary will inform. Why the very last thing Ramsay Macdonald said to me was, Teach them to drink cocktails. It'll help them over many a rough place."

Guadeloupe and Romsteck drank, and were struck chiefly by the extreme icy chill of the draught. It tasted, they thought, rather like paregoric dimly flavoured with orange.

" It seems mild enough," said the President, holding out his glass.

" Only one to begin with," the Colonel advised. " I have seen European statesmen of the very highest rank, over-confident with this mixture, sign away whole provinces. No, Herr President, speaking as your adviser, if you desire to emerge from this negotiation with a whole skin, go easy on the cocktail. Myself, having less at stake, perhaps I may be permitted——"

75

He poured himself a second and handed the shaker to the butler.

" Remove it," he said. " Bring it in again after the Ambassador's arrival."

" Major, is everything in readiness? " asked Guadeloupe.

Romsteck was well aware of the importance of the occasion.

" Yes, Herr President. The American shrub has been generously displayed in Frau Quackenbush's bedroom, and also elsewhere about the house. The staff have their instructions."

" It makes a pretty decoration," said Cointreau, admiring the sprays of goldenrod on the marble mantel. " Just matches my epaulettes. I also instructed Lorli to dress Fräulein Nyla in yellow, which will go well with these trousers. The sword must have been rather a nuisance to Dalmatian admirals. An awkward thing when you're trotting round a dry-dock."

He removed the weapon and laid it on the table.

" And now, Herr President, suppose we run over our vocabulary while we can. Did you study the list of informal phrases I wrote down for you? "

Guadeloupe took out a sheet of paper and glanced over it anxiously.

" I tried. American seems an eccentric language."

" The Americans are an eccentric people.

What would you say if you wanted to express to Herr Quackenbush that something had made a powerful impression on you? "

" Zat gived me a vhale of a kick," replied the President, whose American had a rich guttural and laryngic timbre.

" Excellent," commended the Colonel. " The very idiom. And a phrase of admiration in honour of a lady whom you desired to compliment? "

The President pondered.

" I say, she is hot dog."

Cointreau shook his head.

" I tell ze vorld, she is hard-boiled."

" That might be true," said the tutor, " but not diplomatic."

" I say she have four flushes."

" Wrong again. We'd better go over this once more."

They were interrupted in their studies by Romsteck, who announced that the Ambassador's car was coming down the avenue. The President waited nervously, muttering phrases to himself. Through the doors, open to the warm summer afternoon, they could hear the approaching whir, but above this there rose shrill yells of distress. They looked at each other doubtfully.

" Is it possible that Frau Quackenbush arrives in hysterics? " said the Colonel. " This is ominous for the debt."

" I think it is a dog," said the President. " That same dog that followed me down the avenue yesterday. I recognize his voice." Troubled by this indignity he forgot his instructions, which were to remain in the Blue Room until the guests were ushered in. He seized the gilded sword of the Dalmatian Navy and ran briskly to the front door to drive off the intrusive animal.

But it wasn't the dog. Herr Leutz, pale with trouble, was climbing from the front seat of the government flivver, while inside the car Mr. and Mrs. Quackenbush strove to control a small girl of about nine years who was evidently in an advanced stage of weariness and bad temper. " I don't *want* to go to another hotel," she screamed. " I'm sickantired of hotels. Take me back to Geneva."

" Don't smack her again, Ulysses," said Mrs. Quackenbush. " It only makes her worse. Hush, Treasure. It isn't a hotel. This is where the President lives."

The screams were halted by the surprising sight of Herr Guadeloupe popping out among the assembled footmen with sword in hand. " It *is* a hotel," she whimpered. " I can see the elevator man," and she pointed to the Dalmatian Admiral who had appeared in the doorway. The yells began again when Herr Leutz, after a piteous glance at the horrified President, tried to lift the child out of the

PLEASED TO MEET YOU

car. Mr. Quackenbush seized her savagely and handed her to Romsteck who carried her in and deposited her howling on the floor. A truck, containing at least three times as much baggage as the President and Nyla had brought, drove up behind the flivver. Among the general movement of servants Herr Leutz seized the opportunity to flee. He leaped into the car and was driven away.

With a series of sweeping bows and with gestures rather than articulate words the guests were cajoled into the drawing-room. Mr. Quackenbush, a large, handsome, hearty gentleman, impressively Senatorial in appearance, had not unnaturally assumed both the small man in the ill-fitting cutaway and the splendid figure in naval uniform to be attendants of some sort. Preceding weeks of this his first trip abroad had already been so full of surprises that now nothing could startle him. When Guadeloupe, in an accent enriched by embarrassment, introduced himself and presented Colonel Cointreau as his interpreter, the American envoy's manner was perfect.

" Some baby," said Guadeloupe soothingly, putting out a friendly hand toward the odious child, who gazed at him with concentrated hostility. " I am strong for vife und kiddies," he added with a polite obeisance.

Mrs. Quackenbush, holding the small girl

firmly in leash, had the bearing of a resolute lady accustomed to preside over large Middle-Western women's clubs. The President, scanning her powerful bosomy figure, couldn't help morbidly thinking of her as a dancing partner. She looked prosperous and well-knit, the kind of person who would resent being trodden on.

" Oh, Mr. President," she exclaimed, " do forgive our having brought the little girl without warning, but our Swiss nurse fell ill unexpectedly and we had no time to arrange to leave her in Geneva. I'm sorry she's so upset, but you know what children are, it's such a trying journey. Mildred, make your pretty curtsey to the President, that's a treasure."

Mildred ducked sullenly.

" Please ? " said Herr Guadeloupe inquiringly. He was ambitious to air his smattering of American, but his ear was not quick enough to follow rapid conversation.

" I think this is a bum hotel," said Mildred. " I bet there's no hot water."

" Pleasure to receive hard-boiled Americans to our tender republic," said Guadeloupe. " I tell de vorld." Here he broke down and gazed helplessly at the Colonel.

" My interpretation tell de vorld," he concluded.

" The President wants me to assure you of

the warmth of his welcome," said Cointreau. " He apologizes for the meagreness of his English; I fear that I myself am not perfect."

" Why, you speak *elegantly!* " cried Mrs. Quackenbush. " Such a relief! You know we were *so* embarrassed when we got orders from Washington to come here. Our French is bad enough but our German simply doesn't *exist*."

" Why does the elevator man wear a sword? " said Mildred.

" Hush, treasure! You mustn't be rude. I'm sorry Mildred is a little peevish. She can be so sweet when she's herself. She's not just an ordinary Mildred, are you, treasure? You know she was named for her grandfather, General Mildred of Cincinnati."

" Hot dog! " said the President cheerily, eager to propitiate Quackenbush. " Your maternal vife give me one vhale of a kick, Herr Ambassador. Pretty nifty! Now perhaps she please to undress herself."

" The Herr President overstates his intention," explained Cointreau tactfully. " He does not always mean all that he seems to say."

" He's funnier than Charlie Chaplin," said Mildred. " Come on, boy, take us up in the elevator. What's the number of our room? I want to write my name in the register myself."

Her exasperated parents, already goaded by a long journey cooped in a compartment with their difficult urchin, made a joint move toward her, but at that moment Romsteck piloted in two footmen with trays of cocktails and caviar sandwiches. Mildred eluded the punitive grasp, skipped briskly across the room and seized one of the glasses.

" Gee, I'm thirsty! " she cried, and drained it. " Why do they wear short pants? "

" Mildred! " exclaimed her father furiously.

" She'll be ill," said her mother. " Treasure, how *can* you behave so? "

In all his career as a diplomatist Colonel Cointreau never surpassed his conduct at that moment. He saw that the Quackenbushes were approaching the frontiers of endurance. With skilful suggestion he lured the excited child on to the terrace, promising to keep her amused while Frau Quackenbush could unpack in peace.

XI

" NOW you must have American cock's
tails," said Guadeloupe, somewhat
nervous to find himself left without his interpreter. He drank one hastily himself, hoping
it might cause some sprouting in his small
garden of American idiom. " So much I hear
about your great outlandish contry. Ve
drink to dose Unitarian States, de whole
tirteen of dem."

The envoy bowed graciously. " You mustn't
feel offended," he said, " if Mrs. Quackenbush doesn't drink. She is a leading member
of our W.C.T.U."

" Yes, yes," said the President, puzzled,
but desperately anxious to understand.
" Quite natural after a long journey."

But he could see from Herr Quackenbush's
startled face that he had erred in some mysterious way. He struggled bravely to improve.

" Be quite easy. Frau Quackenbush shall
plenty to drink enjoy. Your liddle offsprings
too. Ha ha, how it leap upon de cock's tail!
Ve onderstand, peoples from de League
alvays some lushers. I tink you like our liddle
contry, Herr Ambassador? "

" I think so indeed. Of course you have very different views from ourselves."

"Views! Ah, for views, Herr Ambassador—when de sun sits down in de mountains, all rosy in de icebergs! Dose icebergs are like companions, as good for Frau Quackenbush as a second hosband."

" I'm afraid, Herr President, you are premature in calling me Ambassador. My nomination hasn't yet been ratified by the Senate."

" It is de same ting," said Guadeloupe, blissfully ignorant of American politics. " Ve so happy to be recognize by America, great contry, rich but honest. You tell your President perhaps, Illyria small contry very poor. Ve soffer pretty nifty in de Var, de Var got our goats good and plenty, I tell de vorld."

" Let us drink to a happier future," said Herr Quackenbush kindly. "These cocktails are delicious."

" Is it not so! " exclaimed the delighted host. " Colonel Cointreau tell me, dat is de drink you Americans use to put hair on de chest. To de generous great Repoblic of Unitarian States! Ich trink auf Ihr Wohl, Herr Ambassador. I spik Engleesch, a liddle, but American is hard-boiled, makes to me a little cuckoo."

" I think you do very well, Herr President," said Quackenbush politely, though inwardly a little staggered by the other's figures of speech. " You have several phrases of quite lively American slang."

" You tink? Dat is my interpretations, Colonel Cointreau. A most singular man. It is de Colonel who introduce de cock's tails, he visit America, he spik all de tongues of men und of angels, dance de folk dance, he is how you say my right hand, I tell de vorld. I vish you talk mid him, he put you vise to everything."

" That is the gentleman in naval uniform?"

" He looks like naval's uniforms, Herr Ambassador, but dat is uniform of interpretations in Illyria. Colonel Cointreau say no officer so important as interpretation who make rich powerful contries understand troubles of poor little contries. Important officers must have important uniforms."

" And the gentleman who met us at the station, that is your Finance Minister? I suppose he is the one with whom we shall discuss the matter of payments? "

The President, painfully aware that Illyria and the United States would be discussing payments for at least sixty years, was anxious to postpone the topic as long as possible.

" To-night I hope ve tink only of happiness. Anodder cock's tail, Herr Ambassador? So ve have arrange for you and Frau Quackenbush a little dinner, mit dancings und lust. Colonel Cointreau he is de man, alvays lusting. So chenial und so nifty mit his feets, he dance mit Frau Quackenbush, he give her a vhale of a kick."

" It's very kind of you, I'm sure. What a wonderful old house this is."

" Ve hope you und Frau Quackenbush be careless here in Farniente, just so careless as you were to your own house. Ve show you all our interests, yes, de pullet holes vere dey shoot at de Grand Dukes, de pilliard tables vere dey lay out de corpses. My interpretation he exblain, he haf de gift of de gab. Like peoples in America he have how you call rubber heels. Alvays so comical, I tell de vorld. Such a charming, he can tread on people's corns und dey thank him for it."

"He'd make a good ambassador," remarked Herr Quackenbush.

Meanwhile the highly praised interpreter had found Mildred not bad company. She was a spoiled, precocious child, and now tired and cross, but this was the first time she had gone walking with an elevator man and she was naturally flattered. The Colonel's artful wiles completed the conquest his uniform had begun. He showed her the moat, held her hand while she walked on the balustrade, made tempting suggestions of future adventures with boats and fishing, and allowed her to carry the sword. Soon she was chattering away gaily. It had been her notion to insist, with screams if necessary, on staying up for dinner, but he tactfully persuaded her that an early supper and bed would put her in better condition for junkets in the morning.

"I guess there's not many Americans comes here to Illyria," she said. She was aware that she had not cut a good figure at her entrance, and with sound feminine instinct she was hunting about in her mind for reasons to re-establish her self-esteem. "I guess may be I'm the first American child that's ever been here. You know, my nurse, in Geneva, she wasn't really sick, she just got nervous prostrations from taking care of me. I can give most any nurse nervous prostrations if I really try."

" I'm sure you can," said the Colonel." It's a gift."

" You ought to be running an elevator in a hotel in America," she remarked. " You've got too much class for an old dump like this. Maybe I could get you a job at our hotel in Washington. I don't suppose you ever get any decent tips here."

" I manage to get along."

" It's nice to have someone to talk to," she said graciously. " Daddy and Mother aren't really congenial to me, and these people over here are such boobs about speaking English. Lots of times I have things on my mind and can't say them."

" Nothing is more painful, I quite agree."

" There was another American on the train, but he didn't amount to much."

" How can you tell when they amount to much ? "

" Well, you're a foreigner, I guess you won't understand. Daddy told me for God's sake to take a walk in the corridor so's he could get a nap. In one of the other cars I saw this man, and he was chewing gum. That's how I knew he didn't amount to much. He was riding second-class, too."

" It's useful to have a way you can tell, isn't it ? " said the Colonel amiably.

" He was some kind of policeman."

The Colonel seemed interested. " That was queer. What would an American policeman be doing, way over here ? "

" He said he was looking for someone. He offered me a stick of gum, but when I told him who I was of course he knew I wouldn't take it."

" Where was he going ? "

" He didn't say, but he was awful anxious to see Daddy. I fooled him, though. I wasn't going to have him wake up Daddy's nap, so I told him we'd see him after the train left Laibach. Then, you see, we got off at Laibach to change, and I guess he went on with the express. I didn't see him on the other train."

88

" Well, you're a great kid," said the Colonel admiringly. " I guess you told your father about it afterward."

" No, I forgot about it till this minute. I had one of my tantrums, and it escaped me."

" I tell you what I'll do," said the Colonel in a burst of generosity. " If you slip up to bed right away, *right away* mind you, and don't bother your father and mother, because they've got to dress for dinner, I'll make you a present of that sword. You can take it to bed with you."

" Honest? " she exclaimed.

" Sure's you're born. Come on now, I'll get Frau Innsbruck to give you a glass of milk and a cooky and you beat it right to bed. Then we can pull some big stuff in the morning."

XII

IT was odd that so brief an interval should
have had so marked an effect on the Colonel.
When he rejoined the President and Herr
Quackenbush, the interpreter's fluent American had suffered an obvious deterioration. He
now spoke with an Illyrian accent hardly less
strong than the President's own. Herr Guadeloupe, however, unconscious of any change,
welcomed him joyfully and prepared to shift
the difficult burden of small-talk to a more
capable linguist.

" Ha, my interpretations! " he said jovially.
" I schust tell de Herr Ambassador ve turn
over new leafs in Illyria. He und Frau
Quackenbush see how ve burn all our britches
behind us."

Herr Quackenbush, somewhat puzzled,
turned to the Colonel, who was deftly ab-
stracting for his own use the cocktail that he
could see the President did not really need.

" Not britches, britches," explained the
Colonel. " Not britches in de sense of panta-
loons, britches in de sense of Brooklyn
Britches. Ve burn our britches in de behind,
dat is to say ve begin a new era."

" The President tells me you have been in the States," said Quackenbush.

" Ach, soch happy memory of your great contry," cried the Colonel blithely. " I drink to it, so. Zose beautiful Statue of Libertine, zose tall Voolvort Building, zose companionable sobvay, ve haf noddings in Illyria to comparison."

" Your ideas of life are different over here," said the envoy generously. " You have charms of your own."

" No, no," insisted the enthusiastic Colonel. " Here ve are poor and bestial. Ve haf soch ambitiousness to be like America; give us de chance, ve be go-getters, back-slappers, cake-eaters, beeg butter-und-egg men. You gif us easy terms on de debt, ve show our gratefulness ve start de Rotary Clubs, ve tear down de old buildings put up apartment housings, ve dig sobvay mid beautiful newsstands and lofely pictures on de magazine covers."

" I can see you have made quite a study of American life," said the surprised envoy.

" It is de civilization of de future," continued the Colonel in his vigorous guttural. " Strong, romantic, eggsiting. Alvays de Herr President he ask me about America, I tell him it is Paradise, de contry of beautiful vimmen vere de hosbands is shot up in an office from nine A.M. till six P.M. Und your Vashington Deecy, soch a magnificence. De perfect sitting-place for a government dat would be chenerous to poor liddle foreign contries. Und your Prohibition, a noble idea: a contry vere no one never drinks, it leave so moch more for de rest of us."

"Some of your impressions may have been a little misleading," said Quackenbush, "but certainly they are very flattering. You must come again."

"He tell you how moch ve admire America?" asked Guadeloupe, who was unable to keep up with the rapid-fire of his interpreter.

"I say to Herr Quackenbush dat all de modern civilization come to us from his contry, de Ford-cars, de movies, de fine plumbings. I say ve owe de Americans a great deal."

This last phrase, which the President could understand, seemed to him ominous, and he frowned covertly to his volatile adviser.

"Now that the United States has recognized the Illyrian Republic," said Quackenbush, turning politely to Guadeloupe, "we shall expect you to send a minister to Washington. Why wouldn't the Admiral—I mean, the Colonel—be just the man? I could give you some telephone numbers in Washington that might be useful to one of your tastes," he added, observing that the Colonel was waving the cocktail shaker to verify its emptiness. "There would be no need to mention the matter to Mrs. Quackenbush."

" Dat suit me down to de terra firma," replied the Colonel brightly. " First crack out de box I be real von hundred per cent American." But the President shook his head.

" I could not spare de Colonel," he said. " He is my four flushes. Besides also, Colonel Cointreau is delicate official on de staff of de League of Nations, Geneva need him near de bedside. He is de midvife for any contry dat is going to haf a baby repoblic."

The conversation was interrupted by Nyla. Evidently the Colonel's instructions had been followed, for she was lovely in an airy frock of some golden tissue. She was introduced to Herr Quackenbush, and greeted him charmingly. But it was plain to that experienced observer that the brightness of her eyes was chiefly for the interpreter. Nor did he even blame her; he too was vastly taken by the humorous young official.

" It pleases for me to meet you," she said in so daintily foreign an accent that the gross jargon of the others was put to shame. " Dat is de speech Colonel Cointreau tell me Americans alvays say to demselves."

What is so delicious as one's own tongue delicately mispronounced by a beautiful woman? So thought the ambassador, and made her his best bow. He turned to Cointreau.

" Certainly you can't pretend that America has any monopoly of pretty girls."

93

" Speaking for de League, I am happy to state dat no contry has monopoly of good fortune," replied the Colonel readily. " Tanks to de brodigality of nature, dere is gonsolation everywheres."

Nyla reproved her father for having kept Herr Quackenbush talking when it was time to dress for dinner. The President appealed to his adviser with his eyes, but saw no sign of encouragement. When the two statesmen had gone, the Colonel began a graceful speech about Nyla's costume, but she cut him short.

" Gene," she said mysteriously, " you understand about Americans, perhaps you can help."

" What's the trouble? "

" I know it sounds silly, but—do you suppose Frau Quackenbush has a secret sorrow? "

" She has Mildred, but there's nothing secret about *her*. And even Mildred has her points."

" Well, there's something wrong. She's making queer noises."

" Who, Mildred? It's that cocktail."

" No, not Mildred, Frau Quackenbush."

" What kind of noises? "

" Lorli says she's sighing and groaning."

" Probably trying to get into her dinner dress. The American women have a passion for wearing their clothes too tight."

" Lorli says she's in a terrible state, tears running down her face."

" They can't run far, not on that figure. Maybe she's heard she'll have to dance with your father."

" But what can we do? It's terribly embarrassing. You know how much depends on this evening."

" She's got nervous prostration from spending the day with Mildred."

" Gene, please be serious. You said the League sent you here to help us, and now when something happens you don't do anything."

" I *am* serious. I never was more serious in my life. You don't know what a lot I've got on my mind."

" But, Gene, you're so clever. I thought perhaps you could think of something. If you could have a talk with her, I'm sure you could cheer her up. You're the only one here who can understand her."

" What's the matter with her husband? "

" If *you* had a secret sorrow, would you confide it to Herr Quackenbush? "

" He knows some useful telephone numbers. But maybe I have a secret sorrow. Nyla, listen, I want——"

" I've got to go and see that Daddy finds his studs."

" But, Nyla——"

95

" If you can comfort Frau Quackenbush, you can tell me about that later."

" Nyla, you little fiend——"

The blue sleeves of the Admiral were round her, but only for an instant. The victory was as brief and fallacious as any of the engagements of the Dalmatian Navy, for just then Romsteck entered, with a petty cough, to supervise the removal of the appetizers.

The major-domo's manner as the footmen cleared away was perfect. The Colonel, on the other hand, seemed somewhat at a loss. He lit a cigarette, studied the bullet-holes in the panel, and then stood with his back to the room, looking off over the terrace. The underlings departed noiselessly; finally Romsteck signalled with another small cough.

" Romsteck," said the Colonel, without looking round.

" Sir? "

There was a pause.

" Could you cash a cheque? "

" No, sir."

Another pause.

" But I'd have no objection to lending it to you, sir."

" Romsteck, are you trying to embarrass me? "

" Impossible, sir."

" This League of Nations business is so uncertain."

" Very."

" I might be called back to Geneva quite suddenly, and I find that I have neglected ——"

" Precisely, sir. I admire you for it."

A pause.

" Damn it, Romsteck, you *are* embarrassing me."

" It does you credit, sir."

Another pause.

" If a couple of hundred florins would do, sir, it would be like old times. Quite in the Grand Ducal tradition.—I felt the tradition reviving yesterday; but I was sure of it when —when I interrupted you just now, sir."

The Colonel wheeled angrily and strode across the room.

" Look here, not a word against the Fräulein, do you understand? Damn you, the grandest grand duchess in the whole mildewed tribe wasn't worth the heel of her slipper."

" That also does you credit, sir," said Romsteck calmly.

Cointreau stared at him and then turned again to the door by the terrace.

" Well, what is it? " he asked presently.

" What leads you to believe there is anything further, sir? "

The Colonel laughed, flicked away his cigarette, and came back into the room.

" Romsteck, I underestimated you. You're a clever man. But there's not much time before dinner. I've got a good appetite, I'd hate to spoil it."

" There is a man here to see the American ambassador."

A pause, and the Colonel studied Romsteck's face keenly. It was properly inscrutable.

" Does he make chewing motions with his mouth ? "

" It might be so described," admitted Romsteck.

" The ambassador is dressing. The man will have to wait."

" Would it not be better, sir, to see him now ? "

" You know very well it is important the ambassador should not be upset. The Herr President particularly wants to keep him in a genial frame of mind."

" Quite so, sir. Therefore I say, see this man now. He is from the American military police."

" Ah. I think we shall need a little finesse," remarked the Colonel. " Romsteck, I believe this man is a dangerous fellow, dangerous to the best interests of a happy evening. I can count on you ? "

" Absolutely, sir. It is quite in the Farniente tradition."

"A glass of the 1865 cognac and two or three footmen, the big ones, would be helpful."

" Very good, sir," and Romsteck retired.

He returned a few moments later, ushering a burly fellow in citizen's clothes, who saluted briskly to the figure in brilliant uniform.

" American M.P., sir," said the stranger. " Sergeant Higgins."

" Please for to meet you," said Cointreau in his best guttural. " I tought all de M.P.'s vere Engleesch."

" Military Police, from the zone of occupation. On medical detail from the Base Hospital at Coblentz. I have to see Mr. Quackenbush."

" I am sorry, M.P., I onderstand Engleesch mid huge difficulties."

" Maybe you can read it, sir. I have an extradition paper here that explains the matter."

The Colonel examined the document, apparently with some perplexity, for he lingered over it until three footmen entered with a decanter of brandy.

" Dere is a photographs here," he said. " Vot a nasty looking gustomer. You hunting somevon, hey? De Herr Ambassador he is fugitive?"

" No, sir, but I need his OK to get co-operation from the Farniente police."

" It is pitiful, M.P., de Herr Ambassador could not be co-operated schust now. His vife got hysterics, his baby got de nervous prostrations, himself is about to try to gollect some

money from de Illyrian dreasury. It is a difficult moment. You seddle down qvietly, visit
de sights, by und by ve see vot ve can do."

" I'm sorry, I got my orders."

" I do not onderstand," said the Colonel
affably, signalling the footmen to approach.
" Anyhow, our old Illyrian osbitality must be
observe. A glass of de 1865 cognac, M.P.,
den ve summon de Herr Quackenbush.—
More dan vonce, dey tell me, dis cognac have
save de state."

The sergeant, much pleased, accepted the
glass and drank with enthusiasm. He was then
surprised to find Colonel Cointreau holding a
small shining barrel at his face.

" Put 'em up! " said the Colonel. " Quick!
No noise about it, buddy."

The M.P.'s arms rose, one hand still holding the empty glass, which Romsteck carefully
took and replaced on the tray. The three
brawny footmen stood ready.

" You dirty Fritz, what's the idea? " cried
the astounded victim.

" Tousand apology," said the Colonel, remembering his accent, " but ve cannot haf
Herr Quackenbush interruptioned dis evening. You take my advices, M.P., and keep
qviet, it is de old Farniente tradition."

The man ducked suddenly and dived for
the Colonel's legs, but the footmen threw
themselves upon him. The struggle was fierce

but brief. It cost the Colonel one of his Dalmatian epaulettes, but the cold pressure of his weapon on the policeman's cheek brought the enemy to terms.

" Sorry ve haf to be so rude," said the Colonel. With one hand he detached his scarlet sash and handed it to Romsteck, who gagged the angry captive. " Dis is de first time de Dalmatian Navy ever see any active service.—Romsteck, take him away. Keep him quiet until the morning."

The major-domo and the footmen led off the bewildered M.P. The Colonel, now that the tension was over, put his revolver to his mouth. On it he played a cheerful variation of the Moating Song.

XIII

COLONEL COINTREAU, resourceful as usual, hunted about the drawing-room for a pin. As he expected, he found one eventually in the long blue damask window curtains. He stood trying to reattach the large golden epaulette to his shoulder when he was startled by a soft explosion. It came apparently from the great hall, a sudden popping sound followed by a faint whistling gasp. It was not unlike the fracture of an electric light bulb fallen from a height; but there are no electric lights in the Farniente Palace. He listened sharply, but nothing further happened, so he resumed his task, attempting to adjust the heavily fringed ornament at its proper angle. He had got it affixed, rather insecurely, when the sound came again, louder. This time there was discernible also a sort of strangled fizzing.

Hastily he crossed the room and flung open the door; on the very instant he was met point blank by a second repetition at close range. This time it was unmistakable: a sneeze, followed by a gulping sob. The mourner was Frau Quackenbush, weeping fluently.

" My dear lady," he cried, aghast. " Vat can be loose, indeed? Lean on my arm, lean on de Dalmatian Navy dat have gonsoled so many unfortunate females. So, so; there, there."

He supported her tenderly to the sofa, where she sank heavily, carrying him with her. In spite of her beautiful silver gown, Frau Quackenbush was a lamentable sight. Her eyes were bloodshot, glazed with tears; her nose red and swollen, her handsome features puffed with misery. She buried her face in her handkerchief.

" Ach, Himmel! " exclaimed the astounded man. " Speak, lady. You haf a pain? Mildred is sick? De gown too tight? Some calamity is too moch bust! "

She shook her head faintly, holding the handkerchief to her face, a small vinaigrette held limply in the other hand. Cointreau respectfully removed the handkerchief hand and pushed up the smelling salts under her nose. She sighed, and then was seized by another sharp convulsion. She trembled, shuddered, emitted a gargling groan and struggled for breath. The vinaigrette bottle clattered on the floor.

" Gott save us! You feel easier? Ve must buck up, de gompany be soon here."

" I can't go through with it," she moaned faintly.

" Vat rascal have got you in dis gondition?"
said the chivalrous Colonel. " Your osband,
he is onkind? I call him out, I schpit him mit
my sword.—No, Mildred gone to bed mit de
sword. I play him a fatal jackpot.—Lady, lady,
tell to me vat is wrong mit your bosoms."

" I can't tell you," she gasped. " It would
offend you."

" Nodding ladies ever did could offend
Cointreau," he declared soothingly. " Alvays
I prepare for de vorst."

She shook her head, and mopped her eyes
hopelessly.

" Is it de sorrows of our little contry dat
bray upon your spirit? De difficulty of gon-
versations mit de Herr Bresident? I imblore
you, Frau Quackenbush, be confidential in
me. Ve be soch friends, ve dance, ve make
insinuations. See, ve haf pretty gustom of
Illyria, vear a favour for friends. You brace
up, not distress de Herr Bresident mit dese
griefs, I gif you my trophy. Please, you vear
it for me?"

He plucked the loosely pinned epaulette
from his coat and offered it gallantly. With
bleared eyes she could hardly see it, and recoiled with a choking cry.

" What is it, more goldenrod? Take it away,
it's killing me! The whole house is full of it.
Send upstairs for my atomizer, I'm suffo-
cating."

A light broke upon the distracted Colonel. Like a man putting out a fire he leaped to his feet, rang the bell, then seized the bundles of goldenrod lavishly displayed in every vase and hurled them through the open door far across the terrace.

" It's my hay fever," said Frau Quacken- bush in a strangled whisper. " Goldenrod is the one thing that absolutely kills me with asthma. I didn't know you had it in Europe."

She sank back against the cushions with another shattering sneeze.

" The maid said you got it for me as a special compliment," she murmured huskily. " So I didn't like to throw it out."

When Herr Guadeloupe and Nyla entered the salon a few minutes later, Frau Quacken- bush was stretched, an imposing contour, on the couch. On his knees beside her the re- morseful Colonel, uttering frantic endear- ments, was pumping the atomizer into her nose and throat.

" Tell me, dear lady, do de nostrils seem any happier? " he was asking solicitously. " Hosh! " he cautioned the horrified Presi- dent. " I tink she revive. She breathe more freely. Open wide, ve spray out de pharnyx. De pharynx, de larynx, and all de mucous membranes. She have a dreadful attack, un- speakable."

" Gott! " ejaculated the President. " An

attack? Is it assassinations, ravishings? Ach, de Herr Ambassador add anoder million florins to de debt."

Frau Quackenbush struggled gamely to her feet.

" I'm better, Herr President," she said hoarsely. " Please don't be alarmed."

" She was very nearly ruined, but she improve," said the Colonel, medicating the air busily in various directions.

" You prefer ve cancel de guests? " asked Guadeloupe anxiously. " Perhaps Frau Quackenbush too sick for de dancings? " he added hopefully.

" No, please," she said. " I shall be all right in a moment. The Colonel saved me."

" But still I do not onderstand vat is happen," said the mystified President. " And how is dis? " he added, picking up the severed epaulette from the rug. " Signs of stroggle? Surely de age of ravishings is gone by? "

" Ve hope de age of ravishings never go by," said the Colonel charmingly. " Frau Quackenbush und I haf our liddle secrets. It is de old Farniente tradition. Hosh now, here come de Ambassador. "

The footmen brought in candles, and a moment later Romsteck announced the first of the arriving guests.

" Herr Finance Minister Leutz, Frau Leutz," he shouted solemnly.

As the company gathered the Colonel devoted himself assiduously to Frau Quackenbush, and by the time dinner was served she was greatly improved and in excellent spirits.

Nyla went into dinner on the Colonel's arm.

" Gene, I knew you could fix things somehow," she whispered gratefully. " What's become of your sword and the lovely red sash ? "

" I gave them away," he said. " I'm giving away the whole outfit, bit by bit. Wear this for me." And he gave her the golden epaulette.

XIV

THE summer moon poured on Farniente
its soft endearing lunacy. The terrace,
where Nyla and the Colonel were sitting out
this dance, was a milky twilight; from the
ballroom came the sweet innuendo of the latest
Viennese waltz. Illyria is haunted with
music. It sounds in chorus from village inns,
it chimes from old belfries, gipsies fiddle
under vineyard arbours, even the cowbells in
mountain pastures cry a queer elvish clang.
The Colonel can be pardoned if in that perfect blend of evening and congenial company
he had laid aside international cares for a
moment. The music in the ballroom ceased;
he took out his mouth-organ and repeated
the air, which his quick ear had accurately
caught.

"I wish they wouldn't play such emotional tunes," he remarked. " It makes the
roots grow so quickly."

" Beautiful, beautiful world! " exclaimed
Nyla happily. " It doesn't make me feel like
roots. It makes me feel like escaping into that
magic paleness, going farther and farther—
on and on and on. Doesn't moonlight make

you feel like that, Gene; almost as though something was after you?"

"I know the feeling," said the Colonel. He played the tune again, retarding it in an absent thoughtful fashion. "Speaking of travelling and all that sort of thing, I've got some important papers to get off to the League. Confidential reports, you know. I ought to let them know that the republic has been successfully inaugurated. What I mean is, I suppose there's a late train that I could send them on?"

"There's the two o'clock. That connects with the sleepings at Laibach. I know, because Daddy had to take it once when they summoned him to Geneva. Gene, you're so conscientious. Couldn't your work wait till to-morrow?"

"Oh well, perhaps it could," admitted the Colonel tenderly. "But the last thing—one of the last things—Ramsay Macdonald said to me was, Get your reports in promptly."

"Please forgive me," she said, conscience-stricken. "I mustn't forget, just because you've been so perfectly darling to me, that you have to attend to business."

"Supposing that you'd never met me," he began earnestly, and then interrupted himself. "By Jove, that just fits the music!" he cried, and played a snatch of the air again. "We can make up some words of our own. Come on now, take turns with the lines."

The orchestra indoors just then took up the tune for an encore. To that soft accompaniment the Colonel sang his first line :

" *Supposing that you'd never met me——* "

" *In that case let's never suppose,*" she hummed in reply.

" *But then you could never forget me,*" continued the Colonel.

" I'm stuck," she said. " I can't get it. Wait a minute—*Our poetry never be prose.*"

" Grand ! " said the Colonel. " We'll knock Irving Berlin for a loop. Here we go : *That is the tragic in every sweet magic——* "

" *Yes, even the fairy tales end,*" she improvised, in a prettily pretended pathos.

Both paused, struggling for the next rhyme. The Colonel got it first, and warbled in a thrilling *espressivo :*

" *So we can't sever, forever and ever*
Let's pretend Not To Pretend."

He finished off with a fine rich flourish on the mouth-organ.

" Gene, you're *wonderful !* " she cried ecstatically. " You're much too good for the old League of Nations, you ought to be a bandmaster or something."

The delighted virtuoso replied with both arms and the one word that was his favourite ejaculation.

" Darling ! " was his simple declarative statement. One word and two arms, he used to remark, could best express a tender crisis.

" I *do* so like to be admired," he murmured, " and I've had so little of it."

" Nonsense," whispered the infatuated Nyla. " The League must be frightfully proud of you, going round making people happy."

" Never mind the League," he said. " Let's forget the League for the nonce. In fact, for several nonces. We'll go off and found a republic of our own. We haven't had that voyage on the moat yet."

But the affairs of state are not so easily forgotten. Others were also finding the terrace useful, though perhaps less pleasant. Herr Leutz, escaped from the dance floor to a tilting ground not less perilous, was strolling with the ambassador. From the ambassador came only a mild fragrance of cigar while Herr Leutz's words of woe were audible.

" Von hondred eight million six hondred and sefenty four tousand fife hondred and tventy fife florin," he was saying. " Blus aggrued interests up to now, blus interests for sixty-two year.—Ach, Herr Ambassador, you call dat gapacity to bay, dot sound to me like de massacre of de innocents. Und if de florin she go any lower ve haf to hire a plomber to hunt for her down de drain pipe."

The tactful Colonel was about to lead Nyla away from this painful scene when a dark

figure that had been peering about in the
moonlight approached cautiously and proved
to be Romsteck.

" Your pardon, Fräulein," he said politely.
" Colonel, here are the dispatches you were
expecting." He handed an envelope.

" Oh yes," said the Colonel, at first a little
annoyed at the interruption. Then the shape
and feel of the envelope reassured him. " The
dispatches, yes. I wouldn't have missed them
for—for a couple of hundred florins."

" Exactly, sir. The Colonel is always accu-
rate."

" A lovely evening, Romsteck. Are all the
guests quite happy? "

" There is one, Colonel, who cannot be kept
happy indefinitely."

" What does he mean? " asked Nyla.

" He must mean Frau Quackenbush."

" Poor Daddy, he's having a terrible time."

" If ve say von million florin a year for
sixty-two year," continued the unhappy voice
of Herr Leutz, " mit an average rate of interests of not more dan von per cent——"

" This is too gruesome," said the Colonel,
and they turned toward the dance.

Through the open French windows they
could see glimpses of gliding couples, where
the fashionables of Farniente did honour to
the occasion. But there were also some whose
ambit would require a bumpier participle. On

those polished timbers the honest proletarians of Herr Guadeloupe's ministry had rallied bravely round their chief. One after another, with despair behind their creaking shirt fronts, the doomed men had partnered Frau Quackenbush in a series of exhausting oscillations. The unfortunate lady, jarred from clavicle to coccyx, wondered secretly whether even the hay fever would not have been an easier ordeal. Now the President, having vainly sought the apostate Colonel, was doing his best. Holding the lady gingerly at a distance, so that he could gaze downward unimpeded, Herr Guadeloupe was too busy co-ordinating feet to attempt small-talk. Save for his automatic repetition " Excuse, I tell de vorld," or his anguished " Sorry to meet you " when they came solidly against the massy postern of some Illyrian dowager, he performed in anxious silence. The orchestra leader, keeping respectful watch on the chief magistrate's timing, made the mistake of trying to help him by halting the music when he went wrong. The unhappy man dared not raise his eyes from the floor except when he occasionally cast a haggard look in search of his adviser. The latter had been only a brilliant migrant in the crowded ballroom, seen sometimes in the distance floating serenely with Nyla, then disappearing again into the moonlight.

So Frau Quackenbush, aware that a few

more such collisions would be fatal, did the steering. The President turned always in the same direction. His brow, fiercely intent, drooped lower and lower upon her generous acclivities until his head almost seemed to teeter there unstably like the rolling stone on its perch of moss. His English had vanished in his hour of need; he no longer could remember any phrase adequate to thank Frau Quackenbush for the honour and suggest recess. When the orchestra paused he waved an arm mechanically and continued his murderous rigadoon so that the musicians were forced to resume. Indeed, as Frau Quackenbush began to suspect, cocktails, heat, excitement and continuous rhythmic gyration had bewitched him into a sort of hypnosis. It began to seem a nightmare in which she was condemned to rotate for ever while a small dervish in dangerously slack trousers drowsed uneasily on her bosom. She herself was succumbing to the unholy vertigo. Her face was flushed, her eyes closed, she had a strong desire to scream. She controlled herself, as I suppose many a strong-minded matron has done in moments of hellish temptation, by forcing herself to recall the parliamentary procedure of the Ohio Federation of Women's Clubs. Through clenched teeth she murmured the sanative and gracious ritual. *Minutes of the Last Meeting. Reports of Committees. Special Business.*

*The Literary Program. Madam President, we
have with us to-day the distinguished British
poet*—Already the Illyrian ladies had begun
to stare and whisper, a buzz of scandalized
sensation to pass round the room. Then the
Colonel, who had seen the crisis, deftly slipped
through the throng. He broke every rule of
high etiquette by cutting in on the President's
partner and unwound the spell by a few
resolute twirls in the opposite direction. One
on each arm he led the collapsing pair to the
coolness of a window. He lent Frau Quackenbush a handkerchief, her own having slipped
too far down to be decently retrievable; from
his pocket he produced the forgotten hay
fever atomizer and sprayed the panting
President.

" Ha! My interpretations! " gasped Herr
Guadeloupe. " Vere are you all dese years?
Frau Quackenbush, you are phenomenon I
never forget. Some chiropodist, I tell de vorld.
Ha, ve demonstrate de Perpetual Motions,
you and I. Gott, I try to keep my eye on your
feets but dey spread like cockroaches. It look
to me impossible you haf only two legs? I tink
you must be quadruped in disguise. Tousand
gratitudes for de agonies of a lifetime."

" You must pardon de Herr President his
enthusiasms," explained the Colonel. " He is
fanatical dancer, he dance till de cows come
home to de nest."

Frau Quackenbush was temporarily beyond speech. The Colonel put a chair for her on the terrace, brought her an ice, removed her slippers.

"I'd like to go paddling in that moat," was all she said for a while.

"Ve go swimming if you like," said the Colonel, always ready.

"That's the second time you've rescued me," she said gratefully. "If you ever come to America I can show you how I appreciate it. As long as I'm chairman of the Entertainment Committee there'll always be a lecture platform waiting for you at the Cincinnati Women's Club."

It was the supreme tribute, and the Colonel bowed, greatly moved.

XV

IN the great hall, under the beam of many candles, Herr Guadeloupe and Nyla were saying good-night to the departing guests. The President looked senile with fatigue. Not the caducity of the florin, nor the anxieties of the American bondholders, nor height nor depth nor any other created thing could much longer keep him from bed. But Nyla, shining in her golden frock, radiated the divine vitality of girlhood. Her dark hair, her lilac eyes, her pretty tinge of excitement, were caught in a mild flush of quivering light. The impressionable Colonel, halting on the curved stair by the portraits of old lords of Farniente, vowed to himself that those painted ruffians had never looked down on prettier neck and shoulders. " I'll bet you never did," he remarked to the Duke Friedrich, whose yellow canvas face looked biliously at him. " Never one so lovely. Or so chaste," he added with a sigh.

" It would be a pity if the Dalmatian Navy never had any sea service," he said to her as she turned from dispatching the last leave-taker. " I have the punt all ready."

Now in the ancient flat-bottomed boat, tilting heavily aft, they idled gently. Low under those licheny walls the water was dark, scribbled here and there with silver where the moon leaked through the chestnut trees. The Colonel paddled softly with an oar, then with the optimism of a true Dalmatian navigator entrusted his vessel to destiny. The small melody of the Moating Song sighed from his mouth-organ. A gradual diminution of brightness in the windows above them showed that candles were being puffed out one by one. In Illyria the gaiety of evening is not blackened at one flick by snapping a switch. Windows extinguish like stars, paling softly.

" It would be preposterous," he said, " not to pay such a night the tribute of an embrace."

They paid it. The florin may depreciate but the Illyrian kiss remains always perfect par, a sterling medium of exchange.

" Pinch me," she said at last. " I guess I've been enchanted into a different world. I thought for a moment you were some kind of fairy prince."

It was too comprehensive to be described as a pinch.

" Let's do this every evening. Your work won't take up very much of your time, will it ? Is this going to be included in your reports ? "

" One has to exercise discretion," said the

Colonel. " Otherwise everybody at Geneva would be after the job. Republics would be breaking out all over the place."

" I wonder if you do this sort of thing because you like it, or because the League makes you? "

" Geneva expects every man to do his duty," he said tenderly.

From the distant cathedral came the boom of midnight, followed by small tinny chimes tinkling in various quarters of the town.

" Those little churches had really quite forgotten the time," said Nyla, " but as soon as the big one shouted twelve o'clock they all hurried to pretend they knew it too."

" I wish they wouldn't make such a point of it. There oughtn't to be any time in a place like Illyria. Nothing but eternity, like this."

" Mention it to the League," suggested Nyla happily. "Darling, you can do anything. You *are* a fairy prince."

The Colonel seemed troubled. Perhaps he remembered that at midnight fairy princes turn back into disinherited cadets, coaches of state into pumpkins. Fairy tales have so many disquieting analogies.

The slow current had drifted them round the North Tower, under the terrace balustrade. All that face of the house lay in thick shadow.

" Gene! " she whispered, clutching him in

119

sudden panic. " What's that? Look, over there on the parapet. Something white."

" I don't see anything," said the Colonel. " Great place for a ghost, though. Surely this house ought to be haunted by Dukes with bullet holes in them. Or maybe the ghost of the florin."

He pushed the boat off from under the wall into mid-stream, where they had a wider view.

" Jove, there *is* something there."

Far along the terrace hovered a glint of white, apparently suspended above the ground. It was small enough truly to be the wraith of the florin. Then it disappeared. There was a splash and a faint choked cry.

" Gene, it's the little girl! Hurry, hurry."

The old punt was unwieldly in the dark. The rowlocks were missing, and though each seized an oar their desperate paddling only succeeded in twirling the craft in a wild swing which brought them bumping back against the wall. The Colonel hastily scrambled up the rough stonework. He would have fallen but Nyla boosted him fiercely from behind. He vaulted the balustrade and ran along the terrace. Now he could see a small white commotion in the water. With a leap he cleared the parapet and dived in.

It was indeed Mildred. Nervous excitement, the cocktail, the uproars of the orchestra and a lively indigestion had made sleep spasmodic. Her dreams were all of the brilliant elevator man who was going to take her promenading by the moat in the morning. She had been put in a room by herself. Thence, after restless rollings in a vast canopied bed, she had eventually sallied out in an almost somnambulist trance which was half fatigue and half the uneasiness of colic. A rearward stir brought her unobserved to the postern door on to the terrace. Here, refreshed by the clear night, her extravagant and erring spirit desired one more tiptoe along the stone balustrade.

With considerable difficulty the Colonel held up the strangling figure while Nyla, groping along the wall, pulled the punt toward them and shouted for help. The dress uniform of Dalmatian admirals, as fortunately few of them have learned, makes an ill swimming suit. The Colonel was heavily sogged by his golden festoonery. He swam laboriously, grasping Mildred by her armpits; her night-gown had parted and gone adrift in his first attempts to seize her. Eventually they got her into the punt. The dripping Colonel scaled the wall, hoisted up the half-drowned child, and hauled Nyla afterward, leaving their shallop to drift where it would. Mildred, after groaning faintly, suddenly ejected several pints of moat and began to bawl lustily.

" I wanted to see the elevator man," she

screamed. " Take me away from this rotten hotel."

Her slippery nakedness, shining skinnily in the dim light, was pathetic and yet irritating; the Colonel, exhausted, sat panting in a trickle, more than half prepared to lay a tingling palm on the chubs of her small bottom.

By this time the terrace was filling with all varieties of negligée. Romsteck, who had apparently made no move to retire, was the only presentable figure. Frau Quackenbush, who had seen her daughter safe in bed only half an hour earlier, came trailing ribbons with a scream of maternal dismay. The President sped out in a flannel nightshirt.

" Gott! " he cried. "Yet anodder attack on Frau Quackenbush? "

The ambassador was shouting inquiry from the bedroom window. He was beginning to wonder whether the post at Farniente might not prove too vivacious for a man of mature years.

" Mildred fell into the moat," explained Nyla to Frau Quackenbush, soothing the sobbing child, and trying to dry her with a handkerchief. " The Colonel saved her.'"

" De child," yelled Guadeloupe to the anxious parent at the window. " He fell drunk in de moat. But not dead drunk," he hastened to reassure. " Gott be tank, I feared it was anodder case for de billiards table."

Herr Quackenbush appeared in pyjamas with a blanket, and Frau Innsbruck with a bottle of the 1865 cognac, the universal specific. In the middle of an admiring circle Mildred was given a hasty friction, then blanketed and carried off. " That bed was too lonely, I couldn't sleep," she wailed. " I want to go to bed with the elevator man."

" You drink de cognac, Colonel," said the excited President. " Happy days, my interpretations save from de perils of de moat."

" My dear sir," said the ambassador, " obviously I cannot thank you for what you've done. But if there's any way I can show my gratitude—anything, sir, anything. You have only to name it."

" De gustomary ting," said the Colonel, rising from his pool, " vould be to ask you de hand of your daughter in marriage. I spare you dat sacrifice. But dere is von little ting."

" Name it, sir, name it."

" You are here, Herr Ambassador, as blenipotentiary to negotiate de debt. I overhear de Herr Leutz say dat von million florin a year, blus de interests at von per cent, is Illyria's extreme gapacity to pay. Vill you promise me, on vord of honour, no matter vat happen, not to ask more dan dat? "

Herr Quackenbush was a little taken aback at this injection of politics into a sentimental scene. He paused an instant. The Colonel improved the moment with a sigh, expressive of bodily weakness and perils encountered. He wrung a small cascade of drippings from his dismal finery.

" By God, sir, I promise."

" Goot! " said the Colonel calmly. " Remember de terms of de promise, vatefer happen. Ve haf witnesses here. Besides, a gompact made among gentlemen in deir nightshirts must be specially sacred. Now I tink I go change."

He kissed Nyla's hand with a gallant air and went trickling across the terrace.

" Mr. President," said Herr Quackenbush, " if you sent that man to Washington as your minister you'd have the United States paying *you* the debt in six months."

XVI

ONE great advantage of stone stairs is that they don't creak. So the Colonel reflected once more in his brown tweeds, as he cautiously felt his way down the iron hand-rail. He was in stocking feet, groping through the moon-light. He sat on the bottom step to put on his shoes. While doing so he had a sudden fright. The major-domo emerged noiselessly from shadow.

" Don't you ever go to bed, Romsteck? "

" I was expecting you, sir. Is there anything I can do? "

" A clean handkerchief, perhaps. I think I caught a little cold in the moat."

" Here you are, sir. Also I've got some dry money for you. I take it that the bills got wet. Wet money seems suspicious, somehow, sir."

" Jove, you think of everything. I dare say you're just rolling in coin."

" Not at all, sir. I took this from Herr Quackenbush's trousers, while he was on the terrace in his nightclothes."

" That won't do. I can't rob the man."

" Certainly not, sir. If you will kindly re-turn the wet ones I'll dry them in the kitchen and put them back in his pocket in the morning."

" You're an excellent fellow, Romsteck," said the Colonel, rising. " Well, no loitering."

" Beg pardon, sir, but are you really leaving? "

" Bet your life I am; and pronto; it's one o'clock now."

" Look here, sir, you stay. We'll fix that M.P. somehow. You're just what we need. We could get up a revolution and make you Grand Duke. Begging your pardon, sir, but all the chambermaids were suggesting it."

" Delightful of you, old son. No, that splash in the moat cleared my head. I was getting a bit fantastic. That's my trouble, they say I'm not quite right in my head."

" None of the Grand Dukes ever were. That's why we were all so happy."

" I've got to beat it. You see, Romsteck, I'm not what you suppose."

" No, sir. I never supposed you were."

" You're charming at dialogue, but there isn't much time. Remember I've got to go all the way round through the subway."

" Through the passage? " said Romsteck, startled. " You know about that? But you can't go that way, that's where we've got the M.P. locked up."

" Sure," said the imperturbable Colonel. " He's going with me. You don't think I'm going to leave him behind to poison my memory with the Fräulein, do you? ''

" Don't go! '' appealed the major-domo. " I don't mind, sir, if you are a bit mad. It doesn't matter. It'll do us good. Please, sir, for the good of the country, don't leave us to the mercy of all these perfectly sane officials. The League of Nations will put it all over us without you to take care of things.''

" Damn it, man," cried the Colonel in vexation, " you're as mad as I am. Do you suppose I *want* to go, to leave the nubile Nyla and the 1865 cognac and all the fun? I don't want to make you morbid, but I'm not here from the League of Nations or the Department of Public Safety or anyone else. I'm just on my own, and the game's up. Come, we're wasting time."

" Very good, sir. I was afraid you couldn't be persuaded. I made up a little packet of sandwiches for you, and a flask of the 1865."

Romsteck handed him a parcel from a table in the hall, then lit a candle, and they set off for the cellar.

XVII

SERGEANT HIGGINS had had a trying evening. The cellar of the north tower is very nearly beneath the ballroom, and he sat there, angry and perplexed, listening to the clamour of music overhead. Disarmed, his gag was removed and he was given supper and a bottle of excellent vintage, but a couple of stout footmen made it plain that any attempt at escape or disturbance would mean the renewal of bonds and bandage. He had all the American doughboy's disgust at being shut out from any merrymaking in which the other sex participated; and through a small ventilator grating high in his prison he was teased by feminine laughters and light whisperings on the terrace. But philosophy and fatigue presently overcame indignation. He helped himself to an extra bottle of the Burgundy stacked in a corner, and fell asleep on a cot bed against the wall. Thus he was spared, later, the amorous chords of the mouth-organ, which would have puzzled him. The Colonel's moating song was only a few feet from Sergeant Higgins's ear when the punt drifted past the tower.

He was too heavily asleep to stir when a key chirped in the rusty lock and the Colonel and Romsteck entered. Cointreau shook him, and he sat up confusedly.

" Well, here we are," remarked the Colonel genially, standing over him with the candle. " The angel of the Lord appears in a vision to the Military Police."

" Aw, quit your kidding. Let a fella sleep," grunted the drowsy M.P., and fell back on his pallet.

" That's no way to greet the angel of the annunciation," observed Cointreau, joggling him again. This not availing, he tilted a few drops of hot candle-grease on to the slumberer's neck, which effectually startled him.

" Buck up," said the Colonel. " Tidings of great joy. Here's the lost sheep, crawling right into your bosom. What are you doing in the wine cellar ? "

" Search me, buddy," said the sergeant peevishly. " I'd like to get my hooks on that bird in the Knights of Pythias clothes. He got me railroaded into this jug.—Who'n hell are you ? "

" I'm the guy you're looking for."

" The hell you are ! Wait a minute, where's my papers——"

" Here," said the Colonel, taking a pulpy document from his pocket. " I'm sorry it got wet. It was the fault of that Knight of Pythias."

The M.P. examined the paper and then held up the candle to look at the Colonel.

" Your hesitation is natural," said Cointreau. " The photo doesn't do me justice."

" I guess it's you. Well, you're under arrest, see? "

" Romsteck, it's a pity you don't savvy English," said the Colonel, turning graciously to the major-domo. " Here, you've been such a sportsman I'll read you the indictment. The description's quite flattering: *Eugene F. Connolly, commissioned first lieutenant ——th Infantry.*—I'm afraid I have no right to the name of Cointreau. I chose it because it's my favourite liqueur. It smells like orange blossoms.—*Cited for gallantry*—here, we can skip that—*Regimental interpreter . . . five foot eleven, 170 pounds, birthmark*—Come, that's too intimate—*curly auburn hair, blue eyes, athletic and agile . . . . escaped from Rehabilitation Hospital suffering from shell-shock, psychoneurotic hysteria and dementia jocosa*—devilish pedantic, these Freudian terminologies, Romsteck—*obsessional fantasies regarding the League of Nations . . . not be misled by gentlemanly manner and humorous conduct of the patient . . . mentally irresponsible, pathological case of great severity.*—Think of their pursuing a man half way across Europe because he's got dementia jocosa! "

" That's what the world's come to, sir,"

Romsteck replied gloomily. " If a man laughs too much they think he's crazy. Consider a person in my position. I haven't dared to smile in thirty years."

" Ah well," said the Colonel, " I regret that there are also more serious items that I have omitted."

" I wish the Grand Duke could have known you," said Romsteck. " He always insisted that the Americans have no sense of humour."

" Come, sergeant, we'll be going."

" Now? Whyn't we tear off a little sleep, Lootenant ? "

" Nix, old son. Sleep is for the innocent and easy spirit. You and I are going to take the companionable sobvay, unhouseled, disappointed, unannealed. Away, away, charioted by Bacchus and his pards."

" You're the guy all right," remarked the sergeant. " Plumb cuckoo."

" Romsteck, you'll have to say good-bye to the President for me. I fear he will be distressed. I shall always remember him as I saw him last, in his manly nightshirt. By the way, here's a souvenir for you. My credentials from Geneva."

He handed over a small scarlet card stamped in gold, which Romsteck fingered curiously.

" The top of an American cigarette box," the Colonel explained. " The most official-looking thing I know. A friend of mine got into the Treaty Signing at Versailles with one of those.—Come on, sport. Back to the nut college. This way to the egress, as Barnum used to say."

He turned toward the hearth.

" I don't like it, that's the Gawd's truth," said Sergeant Higgins uncertainly. " Goin' out in dark night with a crazy man, me without my gun——"

" I say Yes," cried the Colonel fiercely. " Don't be misled by humorous conduct of patient. Get a move on, curse you."

He picked up the poker, to reach the spring of the passage-way; the M.P., misinterpreting this as an offensive move, leaped at him and they grappled. The door behind them opened with a squeak of ancient hinges.

" What's the trouble? " said Nyla.

She wore a blue wrapper and carried a candle.

" Gene! " she cried sharply. " Is something wrong? "

The men stood apart. Higgins gaped amazement at this vision of loveliness. Cointreau and Romsteck fidgeted uneasily.

" I heard talking down here, I was afraid someone was ill. Gene, what are you doing? Why are you all dressed? " She ran forward, seizing his arm.

" Damn," murmured the Colonel with feeling. There was a silence while Nyla studied him anxiously.

"Your pardon, Fräulein," said Romsteck. "The Colonel has had an urgent summons from the League."

"Oh," she cried, "and this is the courier to take your reports. I had such a fright. I was afraid you were going."

"I am going," he said. "I'm sorry, I didn't want you to know. I—I guess they're going to send me to America.—I've had an offer from a publisher to write my memoirs," he added, with a wretched attempt at jauntiness.

"To America? Gene, let me come with you. Gene darling, let me. I'll go *anywhere*. I don't mind roughing it. You mustn't go to a place like that without someone to take care of you. I'll work for the League, I'll do anything."

"Say, Lootenant," put in the embarrassed M.P., "I didn't know there was a skirt in this business. If you'll excuse me, I'll step outside with the janitor."

The Colonel at that moment had no eyes or ears—or arms—for anyone but Nyla. Romsteck beckoned, and the sergeant followed him to the door.

"You'll be O.K. in here, Lootenant. Take your time. I'll wait for you at the top of the stairs."

"Gene, you'll write to me?"

"Of course I will, darling."

"Do you *have* to go? Is the American republic in trouble too? Fix it up and come back soon. Don't get to be too much like an American."

"Honey, I'm sorry, I've got to tell you. I *am* an American."

"I always knew there was something strange about you," she said softly. "Never mind. Come back soon and attend to the roots. Let me have one good look, so I shan't forget."

She held up the candle, which gave him opportunity to glance at his wrist-watch.

"Hullo," he said. "Where's friend Higgins? Well, never mind. So much the better."

He climbed a chair and poked up the visor in the coat of arms. The passage-way opened.

"Gene, must you go that way? It looks so dark and nasty. Shall I call your courier?"

"No," he said grimly. "He had his chance. Don't let Herr Quackenbush back out of his promise about the debt."

"Gene, I'll study, so we can talk American together."

"Auf wiedersehen, Schätzchen!"

"Gootbye, gootbye," she cried into the tunnel in her pretty accent. "Oh, Gene, it vas pleasure to have meeted you!"

And she burst into tears.

* * * * *

"Daddy," she said to Herr Guadeloupe at breakfast the next morning, "how much postage is needed on letters to Geneva?"

THE ARROW

I SUPPOSE the reason why cabin stewards fold them like that, instead of tucking 'em in as bedclothes are arranged on shore, is that if the ship founders you can get out of your bunk so much quicker. The life preservers are up there, on top of the little wardrobe. The picture of Mr. Boddy-Finch, the resolute-looking man with a moustache, showing how to wear the life waistcoat, is on the panel by the door. Mr. Boddy-Finch's moustache has a glossy twist, probably waxed like that to keep it from getting wet while he's demonstrating his waistcoat. He guarantees that the thing will keep you afloat for forty-eight hours: how can he tell unless he's tried it? Amusing scene, Mr. Boddy-Finch floating competently in the Mersey while a jury of shipowners on the dock cheer him on toward the forty-eighth hour.

So he was thinking as he got into the berth and carefully snugged himself into the clothes that were folded, not tucked. The detective story slid down beside the pillow. No bed companion is so soothing as a book you don't intend to read. He had realized just now that the strangeness had worn off. This was his first voyage. He had supposed, of course, he would be ill, but he had never felt more at home, physically, in his life. The distemper that had burdened him was of another sort; but now it was gone—gone so quietly and completely that he hardly missed it yet. He only knew that some secretive instinct had brought him early to his bunk, not to sleep, but because there, in that narrow solitude, he could examine the queer delicious mood now pervading him.

The steady drum and quiver of a slow ship finding her own comfortable way through heavy sea. The little state room, which he had to himself, was well down and amidships; the great double crash and rhythm of the engines was already part of his life. A pounding hum, pounding hum, pounding hum. He invented imitative phrases to accompany that cadence. O lyric love, half piston and half crank! Roofed over by the upper berth, shaded from the lamp by the clicking chintz curtain, this was his lair to spy out on the laws of life. He could see his small snug dwelling sink and sway. Marvellous cradling ease, sweet equation of all forces. He studied the pattern of honest bolts in the white iron ceiling. Surely, with reference to himself, they were rigid: yet he saw them rise and dip and swing. The corridor outside was one long creak. There was a dropping sag of his berth as it caved beneath him, then a climbing push as it rose, pressing under his shoulders. He waited, in curious lightness and thrill, to feel the long slow lift, the hanging pause, the beautifully sinking plunge. The downward slope then gently tilted sideways. His knees pressed hard against the board, he could see his toothbrush glide across the tumbler. He was incredibly happy in an easy bliss. This primitive cycle of movement seemed a part of the secret rhymes of biology. Now he understood why sailors often feel ill when they reach the dull, flat solidity of earth.

The lull and ecstasy of the sea is what man was meant for. The whole swinging universe takes you up in its arms, and you know both desire and fulfilment. And down below, from far within, like—oh, like things you believed you'd forgotten—that steady, grumbling hum. The first night he was a bit anxious when she rolled: his entrails yawned when she leaned over so heavily on emptiness. But then he had divined something; it is the things that frighten you that are really worth while. Now, when she canted, he did not hold back; he leaned with her, as though eager to come as close as possible to that seethe and hiss along her dripping side. It was the inexpressive faces of stewards and stewardesses that had best fortified him. They stood on duty along the exclaiming passages, priests of this white ritual world. Their sallow sexton faces seemed gravely reassuring the congregation that all was calculated, charted, and planned. They flexed and balanced serenely like vicars turning eastward at the appointed clause. He had barely escaped horrifying one of them, his bedroom steward who came in suddenly—the door was open—while he was doing a private caper of triumph at realizing he wasn't ill. He repeated his silly chant, smiling in the berth:

> " Wallow in a hollow with a pounding hum,
>   Pillow on a billow with a pounding hum.
>   Now the Atlantic
>   Drives me frantic,
>   Pounding pounding pounding hum! "

If you ever tell anyone this story, he said to me—long afterwards, when he first talked about it—make it very matter-of-fact. I know that some writers have a way of putting things handsomely, picturesquely, full of ingenious, witty phrases. That's dangerous, because people get a notion that these affairs are only the invention of literary folks.

The first days were very uneasy. He couldn't read, he couldn't bear talking the gay chaff that is legal tender on shipboard, he dreaded the discovery of a mutual friend in Pelham Manor that thrills adjoining deck-chairs. He couldn't write, nor imagine concentrating his

mind on cards; besides, he was young enough
to be alarmed by the warning notice about
professional gamblers. He'd have enjoyed
more deck tennis, but the courts were usually
occupied by young engineer-officers and a
group of girls whose parents, in desperation,
were sending them abroad to school. They
were rather noisily true to type and carried
with them everywhere a toy phonograph, the
size of a candy box. This occult machine,
busily rotating dark spirals of jazz, was heard
intermittently like a pagan refrain. It uttered
such cries as Pan might ejaculate under ether.
Long after the diligent ship's orchestra had
couched themselves it chattered, in dark
corners of the deck, against the thunder of
yeasty sea. Evidently it was hastening its
damsels into a concentric *cul de sac* where they
would eventually find themselves blocked.
There would, perhaps, be the momentary
alleviation of a picture in the Sunday paper
("Among the season's interesting brides"),
after which they would be irretrievable
wives and mothers—with friends in Pelham
Manor.

He paced the deck endlessly in windy bright
September. Weariness is the only drug for
that sea unease. At night the mastheads
swung solemnly against clear grainy sky. Even
the Dipper seemed swinging. Here and there
he paused, in a kind of dream, vacantly

studying the log of the day's run, pondering
on the chart a shoal called the Virgins, or
watching, through a brass-rimmed port,
cheerful people gossiping in the lounge. He
was too shy and too excited to enter into the
innocent pastimes of the voyage. Sometimes
he went into the smoke-room for a drink.
Brought up in the Prohibition era, acquainted
only with raw gin and fusel oils, leprous
distilments, he had never before encountered
honest ripened Scotch. When that hale
benevolent spirit amazed him with its pure
warmth, it occurred to him that perhaps there
is no reason why the glamour of life should
not be taken neat. It need not always be
smuggled about in medicine bottles or under
false and counterfeit labels. But the smoke-
room frightened some essential chastity in his
mind. It was full of women smoking and
drinking. They wore cheese-coloured silk
stockings, provokingly obvious, and their eyes
were sportively bright. Perhaps they were
gamblers even more professional than those
referred to in the sign. One evening, when he
had a bad cold, the doctor gave him some
phenacetin and aspirin tablets to take with hot
toddy. That night he lay stewing in his warm
cradle, submerged in a heavy ocean of sleep,
rolled in a nothingness so perfect it was almost
prenatal. So he told the doctor the next morning, and caught a flash from that officer's eyes.

Both put the phrase aside where it wouldn't get broken, for private meditation. Being diffident, he did not tell the doctor what jolly dreams had swum through the deep green caverns of his swoon. His mind lay on the bottom like a foundered galleon, its treasures corroding in the strong-room, while white mermaids . . . No, they weren't mermaids, he said to himself.

But now I know why the steamship companies arrange so many distractions for their passengers.

As nearly as I can make out, his obscure agitations resolved themselves into a certainty that something was going to happen. But he could put no label on this strange apprehensive sentiment. When you can put your feelings into words, they cease to be dangerous. Now you see, he added, why my bunk was the safest place.

He paused. I think he realized that I didn't see, altogether; and I nearly remarked, in the jocular way an old friend can say things, that if he expected any editor to be interested in this story it was time he got into it something more tangible than phenacetin mermaids. The ladies with cheese-coloured stockings had sounded promising. But somehow, with no notion at all of what he was coming to, I wanted him to work it out in his own way.

After all, it's only the very cheap kind of stories that have to be told in a hurry.

Evidently it would be wrong to imagine that his disturbance was unhappy. For I get the impression that, little by little, a secret elation possessed him: on that special evening when he retired early to his berth, he was particularly certain that some blissful meaning lay inside this experience. For suddenly, at the heart of that unsteady clamour, he lay infinitely at peace. The dull crash of those huge pistons was an unerring music; the grave plunging of the ship was perfect rest. He lay trembling with happiness, in what he described (rather oddly) as a kind of piety—a physical piety.

I wanted him to make this a little plainer, but he was rather vague. " I felt, more truly than ever before, a loyalty to the physical principles of the universe. I felt like Walt Whitman."

I decided not to pursue this further, but in a determined effort to explain himself he made another odd remark, which I suppose ought to be put in the record. " One day the chief engineer took me down to see the machinery. But before we went below he made me leave my watch in his cabin. He said that if I had it on me when we went by the dynamos their magnetic power was so strong that it would throw my watch into a kind of trance. It would be interesting as a specimen of polarization, he said, but it wouldn't be a timepiece. Well, it was like that with me. There are some instincts that it's better to leave behind when you go in a ship. I felt polarized."

It appears that he felt himself on the verge of great mental illuminations; but, as one turns away from a too brilliant light, he averted himself from the effort of thinking. He took up the detective story, but it lacked its usual soporific virtue. And presently, still wakeful, he slipped on his dressing-gown and went for a hot bath. The bathroom, farther down the corridor, would be unoccupied at this hour. On that deck all ports were screwed up, on account of the heavy weather, and it was undeniably stuffy. Several state-room doors were hooked ajar, for ventilation, and as he passed along . . .

" I should have told you " (he interrupted himself) " about the day we sailed from New York, a marvellous warm autumn noon, the buoys chiming like lunch bells as we slipped down toward Staten Island. I got down to the ship rather early. After seeing my baggage safely in the stateroom and looking at some parcels that had been sent me—you know that little diary, ' My Trip Abroad,' that someone always gives you; I'm sorry to have to say its pages are still blank—I sat in the writing-room scribbling some postcards. You must realize what an extraordinary adventure all this was for me. My Trip Abroad! With a sense of doing something rather dangerous, I went off the pier to mail my cards. I remember the drowsy Saturday sunlight of that wide cobbly space; taxis driving up; the old Fourteenth Street trolleys rumbling along as usual, and in a few hours I should be far away from it all. It was then, returning across the street, that I noticed the head of some goddess or other carved over the piers. I wondered why, but I didn't dally to speculate. I had a naïve fear that the ship might somehow slide off without me—though there was still nearly an hour to sailing time.

" A friend had come down to see me off, and we palavered about this and that: he was an old traveller and was probably amused at my excitement. The deck was thronged with people saying good-bye, and while my friend and I were having our final words, there was a bunch of women near us. My companion may have observed that I was hardly paying attention to our talk. I was noticing a gray dress that had its back turned toward me. It was an exquisitely attractive thing, a sort of cool silky stuff with crisp little pleats. Its plain simplicity made it admirably piquant. Somehow I had a feeling that anyone who would wear so delicious a costume must be interesting. I can't attempt to describe the garment in technical terms, but it was draped just properly flat behind the shoulders and tactfully snug over the hips. What caught my eye specially was a charming frill that went down the middle, accompanied by a file of buttons and ending in a lively little black bow. I only saw the back of this outfit, which included a bell-shaped gray hat and a dark shingled nape. I noted that its wearer was tall and athletic in carriage, but my friend then recaptured my attention. When he had gone the dress had vanished. A visitor, I supposed; it was obviously the summery kind of thing that would be worn, on a warm day, to go down to say good-bye to someone who was leaving. But several times, in my various considerings, I had remembered it. I thought particularly of what I called the Spinal Frill and the impudent little twirl of ribbon that ended it. Did or did not anyone who wore that know how enchantingly inciting it was? It must be put there with some intention. But was it the wearer's intention, or only some casual fancy of the dressmaker's? Yet it was there to be admired; and if I had gone to the lady and told her how much I admired it, wouldn't I only have been doing my duty?

"Well, as I started to say, when I went by

that partly open door I saw that gray dress
hanging in a stateroom. It was on a hanger,
its back toward me. It looked rather limp and
dejected, but there could be no doubt about
the frill and the buttons and the bow.

" I was hurrying, as you do hurry when
you go along a public passage in your dressing-
gown, and it really didn't occur to me until
I was comfortably soaking in a deep tub of
slanting hot water that I might have noted
the number of the room. Then I could probably have found out from the passenger list
who she was. But even so, I was glad I hadn't.
I didn't want to seem to spy on the gray
dress: I admired it too much for that; and
also, just in the instant I saw it, it looked so
emaciated, so helpless, almost as if it were
seasick. I couldn't have taken advantage of it.
I dallied in my bath for some time; when I
returned, all the doors were shut."

II

THE following day there was that subtle
change that comes over every Atlantic
voyage about three-quarters of the way across.
Perhaps it happens at the place where the
waves are parted, like hair. For on one side
you see them rolling in toward America; on
the other they move with equal regularity
toward England and France. So obviously
there must be a place where they turn back
to back. The feeling of Europe being near
increased the humility of passengers making
their maiden voyage; more than ever they
shrank from the masterful condescension of
those anxious to explain what an intolerable
thrill the first sight of Land's End would be.
A certain number of English ladies, who had
lain mummified and plaided in their chairs,
now began to pace the deck like Britannia's
daughters. Even one or two French, hitherto
almost buried under the general mass of
Anglo-Saxon assertiveness, pricked up and
showed a meagre brightness. The young
women with the phonograph, if they had been
listening, might now have learned how to
pronounce Cherbourg. Friendships that had

been still a trifle green and hard suddenly ripened and even fell squashily overripe. Champagne popped in the dining-saloon; the directors of Messrs. Bass prepared to declare another dividend; there was a fancy-dress ball. A homeward-bound English lecturer hoped that the weather would be clear going up the Chops of the Channel; for then, he said, in the afternoon light you will see the rocks of Cornwall shining like opals. But the weather grew darker and wetter; and with every increase of moisture and gale the British passengers grew ruddier and more keen. Even the breakfast kippers seemed stronger, more pungent, as they approached their native waters, the grape fruit correspondingly pulpier and less fluent. It was borne in upon the Americans that they were now a long way from home. Hard-headed business men, whose transactions with the smoke-room steward now proved to have had some uses, were showing their wives how to distinguish the half-crown from the florin. It struck them oddly that it might be some time before they would see again the Detroit *Free Press* or the Boston *Transcript*. Thus, in varying manners, came the intuition (which always reaches the American with a peculiar shock) that they were approaching a different world—a world in which they were only too likely to be regarded as spoiled and plunderable children. The young women with the phonograph, subconsciously resenting this, kept the records going prodigiously.

In a mildly expectant way he had kept an eye open for a possible reappearance of the gray frock; but ratiocination persuaded him it was unlikely. For it was not the kind of dress one would wear for dancing—obviously, it was not an evening gown, for it had no hospitable exposures; yet it certainly had looked too flimsy for outdoor appearance in this weather. Perhaps it was a garment too tenuous ever to be worn at all in Britain, he pondered, as the chill increased. Then came the fancy-dress ball, for which he was enlivened by the Scotch and the enthusiasm of his steward, who admired his tentatively suggested costume of bath towels and curtains. A stewardess pinned him together, loudly praising his originality, although she had seen one just like it almost every voyage for twenty years. He found himself dancing with a charming creature who might even, by her build and colour, have been the gray unknown. He had intended to be a trifle lofty with her, for he doubted whether she was his intellectual equal; but neither the cocktails nor the movement of the ship were conducive to Platonic demeanour. He decided to try her with a hypothetical question.

" If you had a gray dress with long sleeves

and a nice little white collar, on what sort of occasion would you wear it? " he asked.

" When I became a grandmother," she replied promptly.

" There was nothing grandmotherly about it," he insisted. " It had a spinal frill and a velvet bow on the bottom."

She laughed so, they had to stop twirling.

" The bottom of what? The skirt? "

" No, at the end of the frill. On the saddle, so to speak—the haunches."

" Haunches! " she cried. " If you were any good as a dancer you'd know they don't have haunches nowadays. D'you see any haunches on me? I'm sorry I didn't get to know you sooner, you're priceless. The music is spinal frill enough for me. Come on, Rudolph, step on it."

So they danced. The second-cabin saloon, tables and chairs removed (she was a one-class ship in her last years), was now called the Italian Garden, a humorous attempt on the part of the steamship architects to persuade passengers they were not at sea. It was used for dancing and divine service, two activities so diverse that they cancelled out perfectly. The slippery floor swung gravely; every now and then there was a yell and a merry shuffling as a deeper roll tilted the crowd out of step and they slid against stanchions and the potted shrubs that symbolized

Italy. The musicians, remembering that to-morrow would be the day to take up their collection, braced themselves on their chairs and played valiantly. Like a drumming under-tone came the driving tremor of the hull, pounding hum, pounding hum; the ceaseless onward swing of the old vessel, dancing with them, curtseying stiffly to her partner, smash-ing her wide wet bows into swathes of white darkness. Then the serio-comic yammer of the tune overcame everything, moving pulse and nerves to its rhythm, repeated again and again until it seemed as though the incessant music must cause some actual catabolism in the blood. You remember the song that was the favourite that year:

" When Katie has fits of the vapours
    And feels that occasional peeve
That cuts such irrational capers
    In the veins of the daughters of Eve,
There's still one elixir
That surely can fix her,
    Whatever depressions may vex—
      Sitting up late,
      Tête-à-tête,
    With the So-called Opposite Sex."

Before quitting, they went on deck for a gust of fresh air. He wondered vaguely why he had not enjoyed more of this sort of frolic

153

during the previous eight days. This, evidently, was what life was intended for: he was as healthily and gladly weary as a woodchopper. Would she expect him to offer a few modest endearments? It seemed almost discourteous not to, when the whole world was so lyric and propitious. But as they rounded the windbreak into the full dark blast of the night, they collided with one of the phonograph urchins, embracing and embraced with some earnest young squire. They hurried by and stood a few moments alone forward of the deckhouse. There was a clean cold scourge of wind, a bitter sparkle of stars among cloudy scud.

" Oh," she exclaimed angrily, " will we never be there? I hate it, hate it, this sensual rolling sea."

She cried an embarrassed good-night and was gone. He remembered the head carved on the piers and guessed now who the goddess was.

The next day was the last. At the Purser's office appeared the notice *Heavy Baggage for Plymouth Must Be Ready for Removal by* 6 *p.m.* The tender bubble of timelessness was pricked. The heaviest baggage of all, the secret awareness of Immensity, was rolled away from the heart. Again the consoling trivialities of earth resumed their sway; though those not debarking until Cherbourg had a sense of reprieve, as of criminals not to die until a day later. The phonograph wenches, regardless of a whole continent of irregular verbs waiting for them, packed the French grammars they had never opened during the voyage, and, unaware of plagiarism, made the customary jokes about the Scilly Islands.

He slept late. When he came on deck in mid-morning he could smell England. The wind was still sharp but ingrained with fragrance, motes of earthen savour. Almost with dismay, as they drew in toward narrower seas, he felt the long plunge of the ship soften to a gentler swing. In the afternoon a fiery sunset broke out in the débris of storm they had left astern; the blaze licked along rags of oily cloud, just in time to tinge the first Cornish crags a dull purple. He avoided the English ladies whose voices were rising higher and higher toward their palates, but he forgave them. This was plainly fairyland, and those returning to it might well grow a little crazed. He saw comic luggers with tawny sails, tumbling in the Channel, like pictures from old books: he imagined them manned by gnomes. He was almost indignant at the calm way the liner pushed on into the evening, regardless of these amazements. He would have liked her to go shouting past these darkening headlands, saluting each jewelled lighthouse with a voice of silver steam.

It was late when she stole gently up Plymouth Sound and anchored in quiet blackness. There was Stygian solemnity in that silent unknown waterway: the red wink of a beacon and the far lights of the town only increased the strangeness. After days of roll and swing, the strong deck seemed lifeless underfoot, while some spirit level in his brain was still tilting to and fro. The good fabric of the ship was suddenly alien and sorry; stairways and passages and smells that had grown dearly familiar could be left behind without a pang. It was truly a death, things that had had close intimacy and service now lost their meaning for ever. Glaring electric lights were hung outside, brightening the dead water; slowly into this brilliance came a tender, ominous as Charon's ferry. He waited anxiously to hear the voices of its crew, the voices of ghosts, the voices of another life. It was called *Sir Richard Grenville*, amusing contrast to the last boat whose name he had noticed in New York, the tug *Francis X. McCafferty*. Then, realizing that the *Sir Richard* was coming for him, he broke from his spell, hurrying to join the drill of departing passengers.

" Stand close about, ye Stygian set," he thought, remembering Landor, as they crowded together on the small tender, craning upward. The ship loomed over them like an apartment house, the phonograph girls and others, making a night of it before reaching Cherbourg, chirping valediction and rendez-vous. As they moved gently away, a curly puff of flame leaped from the ship's funnel. Some accumulation of soot or gases, momentarily ignited, gushed rosy sparks. He never knew whether this was a customary occurrence or an accident, but for an instant it weirdly strengthened the Stygian colour of the scene. It was as though the glory of her burning vitals, now not spent in threshing senseless sea, must ease itself by some escape. In the hush that followed the passengers' squeaks of surprise he heard the toy phonograph, poised on the rail, tinning its ultimatum.

Later, just as he was getting into the boat train, he thought he saw, far down the plat-form, a glimpse of the gray dress.

So, by night, he entered into fairyland.

III

WHAT he remembered best of those first days in London was an extra-ordinary sense of freedom; freedom not merely from external control but also from the uneasy caperings of self. To be in so great a city, unknown and unregarded, was to have the privileged detachment of a god. It was a cleansing and perspective experience, one which few of our gregarious race properly relish. He had no business to transact, no errand to accomplish, no duty to perform. Only to enjoy, to observe, to live in the devotion of the eye. So, in his quiet way, he entered unsuspected into circulation, passing like a well-counterfeited coin. Comedy herself, goddess of that manly island, seemed unaware of him. Occasionally, in the movement of the day, he saw near him others who were evident compatriots, but he felt no impulse to hail and fraternize. The reticence of that vastly incurious city was an excellent sedative. Once he got out his "My Trip Abroad" album to record some impressions, but desisted after a few lines. "I felt too modest to keep a diary," was his explanation.

Except for the left-hand traffic, which cost him some rapid skipping on street crossings, he encountered no phenomena of surprise. London seemed natural, was exactly what it should be. At first the dusky light led him to believe, every morning, that some fierce downpour was impending; but day after day moved through gossamer tissues and gradations of twilight, even glimmered into cool, fawn-coloured sunshine, without the apparently threatened storm. In the arboured Bloomsbury squares morning lay mild as yellow wine; smoke of burning leaves sifted into the sweet opaque air. Noon softly thickened into evening; evening kept tryst with night.

His conviction of being in fairyland, when I come to put down what he said, seemed to rest on very trifling matters. The little hotel where he stayed was round the corner from a post office, and in an alley thereby were big scarlet vans, with horses, and initialled by the King. These ruddy wagons in the dusk, the reliable shape of policemen's helmets and boots, a bishop in the hotel who fell upon his breakfast haddock as though it were a succulent heresy, the grossness of " small " change, and a black-gowned bar lady in a *bodega* who served glasses of sherry with the air of a duchess—these were some of the details he mentioned. His description of men in the subway, sitting in seats with upholstered arms, smoking pipes and wearing silk hats was, perhaps, to a New Yorker, more convincing suggestion of sorcery. But apparently the essence of London's gramarye was just that there were no shocking surprises. Fairyland should indeed be where all the incongruous fragments of life might fall into place, and things happen beautifully without indignation or the wrench of comedy. London seemed so reasonable, natural, humane, and polite. If ever you felt any inclination to be lonely or afraid, he said, the mere look of the taxicabs was reassuring. They were so tall and bulky and respectable; they didn't look "fast," their drivers were settled and genteel. He even formed an idea that London fairies, if encountered, would wear very tiny frock-coats and feed on the daintiest minuscule sausages; with mustard, of course; and miniature fried fish after the theatre.

The region where Shaftesbury Avenue and Charing Cross Road transect in an X, like policemen's braces, was his favourite resort. There was no rectitude in the union of these highways, theirs was a gay liaison that had begotten huge families of promiscuous byways and crooked disorderly stepstreets. One parent absorbed in literature, the other gaily theatrical, the young streets had grown up as best they could. In the innumerable bookshops of Charing Cross Road, he spent October afternoons; the public lavatory of Piccadilly Circus was near for washing his hands, always necessary after browsing along second-hand shelves. Then the cafés of Soho were pleasant to retire to, taking with him some volume he had found. No man is lonely while eating spaghetti, for it requires so much attention. He dined early, to visit the pit queues before the theatres opened. There courageous eccentrics sang or juggled or contorted, to coax largesse from the crowd.

It may have been some book he was looking at that sharpened his ear. Outside the bookshop a street piano was grinding, and presently the bathos of the tune, its clapping, clanging gusto, became unendurable. It was sad with linked saccharine long drawn out, braying and gulping a fat glutton grief. It had an effect, he said, of sweet spaghetti boiled in tears. It was an air that had been much played on the ship, and for a moment he felt the dingy bookshop float and sway. The verses he had been reading may also have had some effect: poetry, pointed so brutally direct at the personal identity, is only too likely to bring the heart back to itself and its disease of self-consciousness that is never quite cured. The melody ended and began again. It was a tune concocted specially for dusk, for the hour when filing cases are shut and vanity cases opened; for the dusk, dreadful to solitary men; and he fled down Shaftesbury Avenue to escape. But the deboshed refrain pursued him, it lodged in his fertile cortex like a spore and shot jigging tendrils along his marrow. The ship, forgotten in these days of fresh experience, returned to his thought. He felt her, rolling the whole pebbled sky and wrinkled sea like a cloak about her wet shoulders; he saw her, still in a dark harbour, gushing a sudden flight of sparks.

"I'll wash my hands and go to a show," he thought.

A golden filtration was flowing into the cool dusk of Piccadilly Circus. The imprisoned fire had begun to pace angrily to and fro in the wire cages of advertising signs. Rows of sitting silhouettes, carried smoothly forward on the tops of buses, moved across the pale light. Black against the shimmer was the figure of a winged boy, lifted on one foot's tiptoe, gazing downward part in mischief, part in serene calculation. His outstretched bow was lax, his hand still drawn back after loosing the string. The frolic knave, tilted in airy balance, gauged the travel of his dart. His curved wings, tremulous to poise him so, seemed visibly to spread and flatten in the diamond air. Along a slant of shadow, where light was grained with slopes of sunset, sped the unseen flash.

And having, as he thought, washed his hands of the matter, coming blithely upstairs from the basin, he received the skewer full in the breast.

The shock thrust him backward upon another pedestrian. " Careful how you poke that umbrella about," someone said. At first he felt dizzy, and did not know what had happened until a warm tingling drew his attention. The thing had pierced clean through him, a little aside of the middle waistcoat button.

It was prettily opalescent, with tawny gilt feathers. Sparkles from the electric signs played on the slender wand; the feathered butt projected at least eight inches in front of his midriff. Anxiously reaching behind, he felt that an equal length protuded from his back, ending in a barbed head, dreadfully keen.

His first thought was not one of alarm, though he realized that such a perforation might be serious. " Isn't that just my luck," he reflected, " with my new suit on? " For only that morning he had put on his first British tweeds.

The horns of buses and cars, the roar of traffic, seemed very loud: almost like a crash of applause, the great shout of a sport-loving throng acclaiming this champion shot. He stood there, tottering a little, suddenly concentrated full on himself. It was surprising that there was no pain. A hot prickling and trembling, that was all. Indeed he felt unusually alert, and anxious to avoid attracting attention. People might think it somehow ill-mannered to be transfixed like this in such a public place; an American kind of thing to do. He tried to pull out the arrow, both forward and backward, but it would not budge; and tugging at it merely suffused his whole system with eddies of fever. Already several people were looking curiously at him. He hastily gathered his loose overcoat, which had been flapping open when he was hit, over the feathery tail. Unpleasantly conscious of the shaft emerging from his back, and which he could not hide, he set off toward the nearest policeman.

As he crossed the darkening and crowded Circus, edging carefully sideways to avoid spitting anyone with his awkward fixture, it appeared more and more difficult to consult a policeman in this matter. The all-competent, solid, and honourable London bobby seemed the last person to whom one would willingly confess so intimate and absurd a humiliation. And as he was not in pain or weakened, but even strangely exhilarated and feeling a desire to sing, when he stood beside the constable he found it difficult to mention the topic.

Without removing his vigilant gaze from the

traffic, the policeman bent a courteous ear down toward him.

" Which bus for Bedford Square? " he found himself asking.

" Number 38, sir." (Or whatever the number was.)

He had intended to remark, as casually as possible, and with his best English lift of intonation, " I say, constable, I've had a little accident, I wonder if you'd help me." But he had a clear vision of the astounded officer halting all the traffic and a morbid crowd gathering to stare while the stalwart fellow placed a huge foot on his chest and hauled out the shaft. He would have to lie down on the pavement; it would be very painful, he might scream. No, it was too public.

" See here, constable," he said nervously, " has anyone been shooting arrows round here? "

Still watching the stream of vehicles, the policeman took his arm in a powerful grasp and held it kindly but firmly until there was a pause. Then he turned and looked at him carefully.

" Not this early in the evening," he said. " Why, the pubs is only just open. Later on, I dare say, the air is thick with 'em. Now, you take my advice, get along 'ome to Bedford Square and 'ave some black coffee."

" Well, look here! " he cried angrily

165

" What do you think of that? " He flung open his overcoat to show the thin pearly shaft and the sparkling feathers.

The bobby gazed unmoved. " Button up your coat," he advised. " Someone'll nip that nice watch-chain." He escorted him to a neighbouring curb.

" Here's where your bus stops. Now, no more o' your nonsense."

The attentive faces of the throng alarmed the young American into silence. He mounted the omnibus, and sat carefully ajar on the outside of a seat, to prevent the arrow striking anything. But even so, three passengers complained that he was jabbing them, and he was put off before they reached Oxford Street.

IV

RETURNED to his hotel, he evaded the talkative doorman and gained the privacy of his chamber. He took off his outer garments though with some difficulty, and studied his casualty. The arrow had caused no laceration or visible injury; it had pierced him as cleanly as a needle would enter a pudding. He was aware of a warm tickling, a quickening excitement threaded through some inmost node of his being. The unreasonable missile had traversed some region more intimate even than heart or brain or anything palpable. It seemed to be lodged in his very identity, in some surprised and tender essence he could only describe as Me. He tried to break off the projecting ends of the dart; but when he wrenched and twisted, it proved strangely flexible though apparently so glassy and brittle. He backed against the window, hooked the barbed point over the sill, and gave a gigantic heave to pull it out. It was immovable, and the effort only left him dizzy and shaken, with flying volleys of anguish that scattered down every frantic nerve. He desisted and sat for a while almost faint while the chair twirled under him and the delicate engine shone and burned and quivered in his vitals. Now it glowed and sparkled with frolic lustre until he was almost proud of so singular a stickpin; now it paled and dwindled until he clutched at his breast to see if it were really there.

He was roused by the dinner gong. Evidently he must make plans to carry on his life with this fantastic inherent. He rang for hot water. When the chambermaid appeared he was standing in his shirt sleeves directly under the light, waiting anxiously to see if she would cry out when she noticed his condition. Chambermaids, he reasoned, are trained to observe anything unusual.

She brought the water, drew the blinds, and turned down the bed without comment. He stood rotating under the lamp so that she could see him from all angles.

"Chambermaid," he said nervously, "I wonder if you would——"

He hesitated, realizing that someone in the hall might overhear. He closed the door. The maid looked surprised, as his previous conduct in the house had given no suggestion of eccentricity.

He wished he knew her name: it would have made it easier, somehow, to call her Betsy or Maggie.

"My shirt," he said, struggling for an easy

familiar tone. " I want you to help me with my shirt."

" It's a pretty pattern, ain't it, sir? " she remarked cheerfully. " Oh, you want it mended, don't you? It's torn, what a pity; you must've caught it on a nail."

" Yes, but how about the back? " he asked, turning. " Is that torn too? "

" Oh, Lor', sir, so it is; a nasty little 'ole."

" Is that all? "

" Well, beg pardon, sir. I b'lieve your undervest's tore too, let me—ouch! "

She gave a squeak.

" What's the matter? " he cried.

" That's not fair! " she exclaimed angrily, rubbing her plump forearm, evidently puzzled whether this was a practical joke or some new method of beginning a flirtation.

His spirits improved at this evidence of the arrow's invisibility. Keeping at a discreet distance, he suggested that she must have pricked herself on some fastening in her dress.

" All I say is, it's taking a liberty to go shoving pins into people that's trying to be 'elpful."

He pacified her by making a generous offer for the repair of his linen.

" You see," he explained, " the doctor says I don't get enough ventilation. He wants me to have a little loophole in the front and back of my clothes—then there'll always be a current of air. Now if you'll do that for me, I mean cut out the holes and hem them, I'll give you a pound."

" It'll be blessed draughty with winders cut in your clo'es," she said. " You ain't seen a London winter. 'Owever, it's your fun'ral, not mine. A quid? I'll embroider them 'oles proper for a quid."

He went down to dinner somewhat fortified. It was the first time he had taken any meal except breakfast in the hotel, and his arrival agitated the head waiter, a small pallid creature troubled by any sudden decision. He had to stand in full publicity while a table was found for him, but none of the diners noticed any oddity in his outline. If they only knew, he thought.

The places against the wall were all occupied; he must take one in the centre of the room; and he discovered that when he sat the butt of the arrow exactly encountered the edge of the board, while the point protruded below the top rail of the open chairback. He had to sit far out, reaching his food at arm's length; worse still, this brought him dangerously near an adjoining table, where the Bishop was. The head waiter, perpetually anxious about offending someone or inadvertently making some blunder in sedentary precedences, presently approached to push in his seat for him. The American foresaw the manœuvre just in time, and leaped to his feet; the servant, very much startled, apologized, wondering what error had been committed. He managed to frame some explanation about a sudden cramp in his foot, and prevented a second attempt on the chair by saying that a leg of the table was in the way. But the waiter, with the timorous obstinacy of his kind, hung about zealously. Already a number of eyes were on them, keen with that specially recognizable disapproval which human beings exhibit when anyone behaves queerly in a dining-room. Even the Bishop, who was doing wonders with some sort of steaming jam roll, looked half-way round.

" It was really damned embarrassing," he told me. " By some accidental recommendation I had fallen into a hotel—or *an* hotel, as they called it—that catered solely to English. A Continental or American visitor was almost unheard of; most of their patrons, as I noted in the register, had such extravagantly British names as Mrs. Elphin-Elphinstone, The Moated Grange, Monk Hopton, Salop. There was even a Lady in the house, for, turning over the mail on the hall table, I had noted a letter delightfully addressed to Nurse Edwards, care of Lady Smithers; you can hardly guess how unco that seemed to me. As for the Bishop, I don't know that he really was one;

I call him so because that was the impression he gave me, but he may have been something even more mysterious, such as a Prebendary. Anyhow, in those first days I had been pleasantly aware of having slipped by good hazard into a pure tissue of England. I had been faced by unfamiliar questions, propounded with sacred solemnity, as when that fool waiter would ask if I wanted thick soup or clear; or my coffee black or white; or sweet or savoury? But I had successfully disguised my excitements, happy just not to be noticed. Now this was all ended. The villainy of chance had marked me with a stigma sure to make me grotesque, and not even pitiable because it could not be seen. I wondered desperately, as I carefully conveyed my soup in long trajectory toward my mouth, whether a cube of that solid Yorkshire pudding of theirs could be used as a buffer on the point of my arrow, to prevent the waitress from spearing herself. She was an enthusiastic girl and kept rushing toward the narrow space between my chair and the Bishop's with relays of brussel-sprouts or stewed cheese; and each time I had to turn hurriedly and reach for whatever she brought before she could get behind me.

" In this morbid sharpening of my senses, I'm afraid I may have returned a little resentfully the gazes that came my way. The fact is, I was studying the other guests more closely than before. I envied them their perfect adaptation to the scene, their rich normality, their subconscious certainty that what they were doing was regular and right. They could not possibly have guessed that their fresh gobbling voices, their simultaneous use of knife and fork, the actual food they ate and clothes they wore, were all astounding to me: they were happy, bless them, because they were unaware of themselves, just as I had been; their tender psyche was not spitted like an unchloroformed butterfly. I thought bitterly how mad a man is to come abroad, for it makes him sensible of the strangeness of life instead of merging undissenting into it, which is the only peace. But queerer still: as soon as *my* behaviour became indecorously odd, as it now unavoidably was, they seemed more cordial. I suppose that in some way the report had gone round that I was an American; well, as long as my demeanour was indistinct from that of any other well-behaved young man, they were gently disappointed; but when I showed signs of strangeness it satisfied some vague notion in their minds. And in the oblique profile of the Bishop, as I glanced over my shoulder, I could divine the enigmatic radiation of a man who is about to say something. I watched him apprehensively, and when he pushed his chair back, I got hastily to my feet. He seemed surprised at

173

what he can only have thought an excessive courtesy; but he had his cup in his hand and asked me, most charmingly, if he might take coffee at my table.

" I may as well admit that he captivated me at once. I had thought, watching him a few times at breakfast, that there was a certain ludicrous discrepancy between his clean-shaven austerity and the extreme gusto with which he approached his food and his morning *Times*. I could imagine him removing from his mind things in the paper that disagreed with him just as efficiently as he set aside bones in his haddock. But, after all, I don't know why a bishop shouldn't enjoy his meals as heartily as anyone else. And here he was, the star boarder, in pure goodness of heart taking pains to be gracious to a young alien. His clear gray eyes were so magnificently direct, it seemed incredible he should not see my gruesome predicament. In pursuit of theological niceties he must have accepted without question many paradoxes just as puzzling as my arrow; but he showed no sign. I yearned to confess my trouble. Who better than a bishop should be able to understand and console my difficulty? But, curiously, I saw in him the same ruddy benign solidity, the same aversion from surprise that had made it difficult to appeal to the policeman. I suspected that he was being kind to me on the tacit understanding that I would behave more or less as he expected me to; and I made a resolute attempt to hide my distress. I tucked my napkin over the hole in my waistcoat and welcomed him as courteously as possible.

" ' I trust you won't think I'm intruding,' he said, ' but I heard you were an American going up to Oxford, and as an old Oxonian myself I wanted to wish you luck. I suppose you are a Rhodes Scholar? '

" I assented.

" ' I met a most charming Rhodes Scholar once, also from Ohio,' he continued. (I wish you could have heard his genial pronunciation of the word, equally accenting all three syllables.) ' A fine, manly fellow. It has been an excellent thing for the old Varsity to have so many young Americans; you seem to bring us a freshness of outlook, vigorous high spirits that we need.'

" I feared inwardly that he must be disappointed in me as an example of high spirits.

" ' I suppose you have already graduated from some American university,' he said. ' I wonder if it could be Princetown? I had a friendly invitation from there at one time, to lecture in the Divinity School. No? Having taken a degree already makes your men a little more mature in some ways than our undergraduates.'

175

" I explained that I was twenty-two. I did not insist how considerable an age it then seemed.

" ' Which college are you going to at Oxford? ' he asked.

" ' St. John's.'

" 'Ah, quite one of the best. You will be very happy there. Trinity was my shop, but I often used to go to St. John's for meetings of the Archery Club. Perhaps you didn't know that there's great enthusiasm at St. John's about their historic Archery Club. They have marvellous lunches and then go out in the garden to shoot with bows and arrows. Sometimes, when the lunch has been excessive, it's a bit dangerous, arrows flying round all over the place. But it's quite the leading club at John's; it would be an amusing experience for you if you were elected.'

" I was far too depressed to enter with much enthusiasm into the notion of the Archery Club, or tell him that I would make a singularly appropriate member. I was realizing that, of course, my whole Oxford career, so eagerly anticipated, was completely blighted. Undergraduates, more than any others, are children of conformity, and anyone so cruelly unique must necessarily be a pariah. I mumbled doleful replies while he chatted kindly on. But the arrow fretted me with stealthy fire, and the cleric's amiable regard became rather pebbly. His was an established mind, neatly reticulated into a seemly satisfying world; the slightest whisper of my furious fancies would have pained him unspeakably. The obvious necessity for concealing everything I was really thinking about made me gloomy and solemn.

" ' I'm glad you approach your studies in a serious spirit,' he said finally. ' You won't be wasting your time in mere pranks.'

" He finished his coffee and rose. Sunk in private misery, I forgot to rise with him. He turned to pick up his napkin from the next table, and standing so backed directly on my naked barb. It reached him blithely in the postern, honouring him in the breech as Hamlet might have said; that chub elastic region certainly had not been so invaded since he was an urchin at school. At the moment I was absently finishing my savoury; when I heard him leap and yell I turned aghast; he, seeing me fork in hand, can only have thought I had wantonly prodded him in sheer overplus of savagery. The head waiter came running; the other guests stared to see the admired prelate distractedly chafing his postremity and glaring excommunication. ' Let me explain,' I cried wildly, ready to confess all and cast myself on his mercy; but the very phrase condemned me. I will not elaborate the dreadful scene. I still remember the face of the head waiter. If it had been Mrs. Elphin-Elphin-stone herself who had been impaled, he could not have been more scandalized. There was only one decency possible. I packed, paid my bill, called a taxi, and sought another lodging. It occurred to me, in the cab, that perhaps I should have sent for Nurse Edwards, care of Lady Smithers, and offered to pay for a compress or tourniquet. But a tourniquet would have been awkward."

V

A LONG and restless night gave ample opportunity for meditation. Sleep was difficult: he had to lie accurately on edge, and could not turn over on the other side without first getting out of bed. If he dozed into peaceful oblivion some uncanny movement would jar the weapon and bring him back to his affliction. There it was, fantastic, inextricable, struck through the very pulse of his consciousness. Besides being infernally uncomfortable, the thing suggested further privations. A life of celibacy, for instance—a thought distasteful to young men. If it had not been for a bottle of brandy in his luggage he would hardly have slept at all; but he discovered that generous potations seemed to dull the point of the shaft and make it smaller. A lukewarm consolation crept into his mind: perhaps everyone else was also concealing some equally embarrassing anguish—a secret that perhaps did not take the same awkward shape, but was just as disturbing.

The following day the arrow baffled him by showing itself strangely variable. As he slunk shamefully from his lodging it seemed as big

THE ARROW

as a harpoon; he hailed a taxi, to avoid any
possible collision, and went to the Express
Company. There, after a difficult time standing sideways in the line of people pressing
vigorously towards the teller's grill, he managed to cash a cheque. He was leaving, in-
tending to visit an American doctor, when
he was greeted by an old crony who came
boisterously forward. He dodged behind a
pillar and extended his hand warily. His
friend, thinking this a drollery of some sort,
laughed gaily and peered round the column.
" What's on your chest? " he cried, noting the
furtive behaviour. The sufferer's hand flew to
his wishbone, but the remark was purely accidental, for the encumbrance had now shrunk
to such modest size that he could lap his
overcoat over the feathery butt and guard the
rearward point by covering it with one gloved
hand behind his back. Encouraged, he postponed medical consultation and, as his friend
would not be shaken off, they lunched together. For a couple of hours, when he privily
rummaged in his bosom, he could have sworn
there was nothing there. Yet it returned again
later, pricking him with impossible suggestions, so that he had to stand apart round less
frequented street corners, struggling to master
the glittering thing by strong force of will; or
else hire a taxi and ride expensively secure
until it shrank to manageable dimension.

But, without committing himself in any way, he had learned from his friend one fact which promised to be helpful. At the American Embassy there was a young man employed who was, as the customary tautology has it, a fraternity brother of theirs. This means that the young official was bound, by some juvenile severities of their Greek-letter union, to mutual succour in distress. So in one of the ante-rooms of the Embassy's business office we see the stricken one mysteriously consulting this fellow Hellenist. There was an exchange of passwords as Greek met Greek, though not in any accent approvable by Liddell and Scott; and the visitor displayed, for identification, a generous sheaf of testimonials from Middle-Western pastors and pedagogues. With these muniments Rhodes Scholars are always plentifully provided. The attaché, who, with spats and cutaway and a conviction that no gentleman sallies abroad without a cane, had also put on a certain fatigue of the homeland simplicities, glanced hastily through the assurances that his brother was of modest and winning nature, a fine influence in the Christian life of the community, a brilliant scholar, a leader of glee clubs, and a triple-threat halfback. He noticed that, in spite of these resources, the caller looked somewhat haggard, exhaled a faint vapour of cognac, and had a curious habit of standing averted, holding one arm doubled back behind his shoulders. He prepared himself with several irrefutable reasons why the Ambassador was not at liberty.

" See here," said the caller, in whom after several days of wretchedness the sentiment of anger was now uppermost, " is this the place to file a complaint against the British Government? "

The young diplomat was fully aware that complaints against the British, or any other government, were rarely efficacious. And his promotion, slow at best, depended largely on his finesse in preventing the channels of communication from being choked with the assorted woes of American travellers. Accordingly he had framed a polite theorem for the various emergencies of his bureau, to the effect that the United States Government, though undoubtedly a sovereign power, cannot safeguard its citizens against all the miscellaneous vexations of life. This apothegm, though frequently in use, he was always able to utter as if freshly inspired for the immediate instance. It was ready to his lips, but something in the manner of his inquirer led him to a more comradely candour.

" Why, yes," he said, " if necessary. But I doubt if it'll do much good. And it depends on the nature of the complaint. If it's an income tax——"

" It's no use my trying to explain. You wouldn't believe me. I've been to a doctor and all he can suggest is that it's a case of *hyperæsthesia sagittaria*. He's delighted about it, but then he doesn't have to live with it."

" You'll pardon me, I'm sure," said the attaché, " but if you can state the nature of the grievance——"

" I've drawn up a document about the whole affair," said the plaintiff, producing a manuscript. " Now, remember, this is entirely confidential except as regards official channels. But it's the only recourse I have. If you'll run your eye over this——"

The clerk read:

WHEREAS —— ——, a citizen of the United States of America, 22 years of age, residing temporarily at 18, Torrington Square, London, desires to make complaint against H.M. Government as follows:

Whereas on the 3rd day of October instant, about the hour of five P.M., the said ——, on his lawful occasions and peaceably pursuing his own concerns, was walking through Piccadilly Circus, when a missile nearest describable as an arrow, projected by person or persons unknown, did so strike and transfix the body and soul of said —— that he has thereafter gone in peril of his life and wits. And whereas the said arrow is not by any ascertainable means removable from the body of the plaintiff, and whereas it has afflicted him grievously in mind, body, and estate, subjecting him to extreme humiliations and necessitating medical treatment for a highly nervous and excited condition and repeated hire of motor taxicabs to prevent embarrassing H.M. subjects on the sidewalks; and whereas the petitioner feels his future

183

career and tranquillity gravely compromised by this affliction, he respectfully submits that it is the plain duty of H.M. Government, acting through the London County Council or any other lawful body, to keep the region of Piccadilly Circus free of such random projectiles and that neglect of such precautions has resulted in a delict upon the person of a citizen of the United States.

Your petitioner therefore prays that damages be awarded commensurate with the offence, and that the American Ambassador in London be instructed to make representations to that end to the officers of H.M. Government.

" But I don't see any arrow," objected the fraternity brother.

"Hush! Not so loud!" said the petitioner, looking round nervously at several other citizens who were waiting their turn to make complaints. He leaned across the counter and whispered hoarsely.

The clerk seemed a little shocked. He read the document again and privately concluded that the Ohio chapters of Nu Nu Phi ought to be more careful in their elections. But one business of an embassy is to allow Time to anoint its healing lotion upon human abrasions, and he fell back on sound governmental principles.

" Well," he said, " I'll put this through the proper routine. But don't expect questions to be asked about it in Parliament next week. First it'll have to go before some Congressional committee in Washington, I suppose, and when they see the word *arrow* they'll probably refer it to the Bureau of Indian Affairs. Also, it must pass through our legal department here, to be put in correct form."

But he was almost ashamed of his flippancy when he saw the exalted earnestness of the other man.

" Did you ever have a secret so important," asked the caller, " that no one could possibly be told, and yet everyone knew it anyhow? "

" Why, sure; that's what embassies are for, to deny that sort of thing." As he spoke he thought anxiously of his own secrecies: private experiments with a monocle that he had never dared wear publicly, and that it was near closing time and he had an engagement to meet a young lady for tea at Rumpelmayer's.

" Put your hand here," the caller said, opening his overcoat.

The attaché did as directed. He felt a sharp sting and a warm hypodermic sparkle snaked up his arm. For an instant he was giddy, the office behind him with its terraced filing cases seemed to rock and grow dim. He clung to the counter as to the bulwark of a ship. He heard music faintly played, the light chatter of voices, and in a brightness soft as candleshine he saw the face of the damsel at Rumpelmayer's.

He steadied himself, fixing his mind on the

tight-lipped engraving of George Washington.

"Really, you know . . . sorcery . . . I'm not sure that this comes under the scope of this office."

The impatience of several ladies waiting attention began to be audible.

"Do what you can," said the plaintiff, and repeated the covenant of their Greek-letter federation. He left, making a wide zigzag to give the other clients a safe offing. The attaché, concealing behind the counter a hasty glance at his wrist watch, assigned two elderly ladies to a confrère and selected the younger one for himself. The only consolation in this job, he reflected, was that perplexity did sometimes descend upon travelling citizens who were really attractive; but even so, not as alluring as the graceful creature who would soon be in St. James's Street, taking her tea and pastry with only one hand.

VI

THE plaintiff in Torrington Square was
surprised to receive, a few days later, a
letter from the American Embassy. It was
embossed with the official seal of the United
States, which he was startled to observe con-
sisted of an eagle with excessively straddled
legs one of which held a cluster of arrows and
the other a foliage that he took to be an olive
bough. Arrows, he thought ironically, he could
supply for himself; the message, written in the
attaché's own hand, was evidently intended to
be of the nature of the olive branch. It was
informal and cordial.

" Your statement," he read, " is having due
attention. I have been thinking about the
matter and, speaking as a friend and brother
in old Nunu, I believe perhaps you take it too
seriously. I think that when you get up to
Oxford the pleasant surroundings of that
peaceful place will soon remedy the condition;
in the meantime I suggest that you enjoy some
innocent diversion. Nothing is more entertaining than a professional Anglo-American
Hands Across the Sea meeting, so I am en-
closing a ticket to the annual luncheon of the

Atlantic Harmony. You will find this well worth attending, Lord Aliquot is to take the chair and Admiral Stripes, U.S.N., will be one of the speakers. Yours cordially."

The date set for the luncheon was the day before he would leave for Oxford. He decided to go.

The attaché was right: one of those meetings at which the two chief branches of the Anglo-Saxon race convene to confess their mutual esteem is indeed fruitful study for the pensive. The Atlantic Harmony lunched in the ballroom of a huge hotel; behind the high table the banners of both nations were draped and blended; an orchestra in the gallery burst into traditional airs; cocktails began and champagne followed. Dishes sacred to England and America were on the menu, and judging by the notable bulk of most of the ladies, there was no danger of the race perishing of starvation. It was an orgy of friendly sentiment; for the time being the Atlantic Ocean seemed a mere trickle; one had to remind one's self that only the fortunately high rate of steamship fares prevented two mutually infatuated populations from putting their affections to the proof *en masse*. Even a man with a serious gravamen pending against the British Government could not resist the general infection of good will. He waited in the lobby until the crowd had gone in, which made it possible to reach his seat without spiking anyone; and by the time the wine had made a few circulations he was in excellent humour. Contemplating the worthy people who are drawn by irresistible magnetism to affairs of this sort, he began to wonder what was the law forbidding Anglo-American friendship to be endorsed by the young and slender. The ladies were mostly silvery and, in the case of his immediate neighbours, deaf; and the gentlemen solid; but their enthusiasm was terrific. References by Lord Aliquot to the Mother Country, cousins, blood thicker than water, the critical days of 1917, the language of Shakespeare, Magna Charta, Your Great President, were received with instantaneous crashes of applause. Admiral Stripes, forgetting the extreme efficiency of the submarine cables, very nearly made Lord Aliquot a present of the United States Navy. Lord Aliquot, after humorously remarking that he himself had made the supreme sacrifice for Anglo-American union by marrying an American wife, insisted that nothing could go seriously wrong between two nations nurtured in the same sense of fair play and reverence for pure womanhood. His Lordship, an old hand at these affairs, took care to end each paragraph with an obvious bait for applause. This gave him time to be quite sure that the next one would not contain anything regrettable. An

American minister, chaplain of the Harmony, offered a prayer for all branches of the English-Speaking Peoples, on whom heavier than elsewhere rests the great burden of human liberty. If any Frenchman had been taken, manacled, into the room, and compelled to listen to the speeches, he would have ended in convulsions. In short, it was one of those occasions, familiar to statesmen, that cannot possibly do any harm and offer a hard-working nonconformist parson a free meal and an opportunity to address the Deity in public. Meanwhile, the Swiss and German waiters scoured about busily, the champagne flowed, and when " Dixie " was played, many who had never seen a cotton field scrambled up and shouted in pure hysteria.

During the halloo that followed " Dixie " he rose and cheered with the rest. Then he saw, sitting opposite across the large round table, a girl who had been hidden from him by a bushy centrepiece of flowers. She was dark, with close-cropped hair; a little absent-looking, as though she did not take this luncheon very seriously; she had a cloak thrown over her shoulders. He was just raising his glass, with a vague intention of toasting the universe at large, when he caught her gaze. They studied each other solemnly, as becomes strangers crossing unexpectedly in so large a waste. Then, in the flush of the moment, he smiled and lifted his glass. She reached for hers, and they drank, look to look. Then, a little embarrassed, he sat down.

But something in her face or gesture fretted him, bothered him as does a cut-off telephone call; he was waiting and wondering. He tried to get another glimpse of her, but the floral piece was impenetrable. There was no time to lose: one of the neighbouring matrons was asking him what was that music which had just been played, and the chairman was already hammering for silence. He stood up again for one more look, and saw that the man on her left, elevated by champagne and the gallant megalomania of the occasion, was still erect and vocal. He also saw how far back she sat from the table. Her hand, stretched out at arm's length, still lingered on the wine-glass stem.

He ran round to her side of the table, and seized the joyful gentleman. " Quick! " he said. " They want us to change places. Makes it more sociable! " The other gaily assented, and took his place between the two dowagers; nor did he ever discover their infirmity.

" Aren't you warm with that cloak on? " he asked. " Can I take it off for you? "

Her quick little movement of alarm, drawing the wrap closer round her, showed him he had not made a mistake. But he did not pause to wonder at his certainty. Shy as he had

always been, now it was as though he looked
at a woman for the first time, and saw not the
strange capricious nymph of legend but the
appealing creature of warmth and trouble,
ridiculous as himself. Perhaps it was the grotesque pangs of the previous days that had
tutored him. Terror of other human beings
had vanished; his blemish was not shameful
but something to be proud of; and his next
words were divinely inspired—they were brief
but exactly right.

" You darling," he said.

The clapping that followed was probably
intended for the Viscount Aliquot, but it came
too pat to be ignored.

" And that's the first thing that's been said
here that was really worth applause," he
added.

She looked at him steadily, something in
her eyes that might once have been terror
changing into amusement; and then returned
her gaze to Lord Aliquot, who seemed very
far away, gesticulating at the other end of the
great room. " You mustn't talk while people
are whispering," she said.

She couldn't possibly have been any different, he thought triumphantly. He had a strong
conviction that those dark eyebrows, the delightful soft stubble at the base of her boyish
neck, that wistfully shortened upper lip had
always been growing and curving like that

just intentionally for him. He was waiting hopefully (as was Lord Aliquot) for Lord Aliquot to be interrupted by another round of applause.

" Of course the proper thing to say," he murmured, " would be, Haven't we met before somewhere? But it's more important to know, When are we going to meet again? "

" We haven't parted yet."

" Splendid. But are you going to listen to me or to the speeches? "

" Evidently I can't do both."

" Well, there'll be a National Anthem soon; I can feel it coming. They'll all stand up, and we can slip away. Besides, it always embarrasses me to sing ' The Star-Spangled Banner ' before strangers. Let's go and have tea somewhere."

" But we haven't finished lunch yet."

" Don't let's waste time. I've got to go to Oxford to-morrow. By the way, if you had a gray dress with a little frill down the back, on what sorts of occasions would you wear it? "

" Why, right here; but I can't, it's got a hole in it."

He leaned toward her, to whisper something, and the ends of their arrows touched. There was a clear puff of sparkling brightness, like two highly charged wires making contact. Some weary guests at the speakers' table brisked up and felt their cravats, believing the time for the flashlight pictures had come. Lord Aliquot, taking it for some sort of signal, called the company to their feet for the American Anthem.

" Hurry! if we wait they'll get beyond the words they know, then everyone will spot us beating it."

They reached the door before anyone except Lord Aliquot had got beyond " What so proudly we hailed."

" ' What so proudly we hailed,' " he said, as the words pursued them into the lobby " That suggests taxies. Let's grab one."

VII

"ANTHEM? Nonsense, we've just had one."

But then they saw the old fellow meant a hansom. There it was, drawn up by the——

"Bet you don't know how they spell curb over here," he said as they climbed in. "They spell it K E R B. You know it's the first time I ever rode in one of these things. Who's that talking to us from the sky?"

They looked up and saw a curious portrait floating upside down above them. It was framed in a little black square, like an old Flemish master—the colour of Tudor brick grizzled with lichen. It proved to be the face of the lisping cabby.

"Oh, anywhere where one does drive in London."

"I want to see the Serpentine," she said. "I'm always reading about it."

"Very good, mith." The brick portrait floated a moment genially and then said with bronchial jocularity, "Adam and Eve and the Therpentine." They laughed—the sudden perfect laughter of those overtaken unawares by the excellence of the merry-making world.

The cab tilted, jingled, swayed off, rolling lightly like a canoe.

" Of course this is simply magic. Things just don't happen like this," he said as they settled themselves. " Are you comfortable? If I put my arm round you, it would prevent the point of yours from punching into the seat. You see, I can sit sort of diagonal, and then if you slide over this way——"

" It gives me a spinal frill when it touches anything," she admitted.

He looked at her amazed.

" Yes, that girl on the ship told me what you said. She was my room-mate."

" Why didn't I ever see you on board? "

" You did, but you didn't look at me."

" I'll make up for it now."

" Besides, I was ill. Not just seasick ill, ill in my mind. Don't let me go in a ship again— it's too elemental."

The tips of the two arrows touched, and again there was a little fizzing flash. Just the thing for lighting cigarettes, they found, and practised it.

" As a matter of fact I have two arms," he added presently.

" The dusk comes early in London," she said.

" You darling," he repeated, saying it with the accent that can only be uttered in a hansom.

" I think mine's loose," she said. " It seems to waggle a little."

" Mine doesn't bother me a bit as long as we sit like this."

" I thought I was mad."

" So did I. Now I know it. I went to an astrologer, one of those fellows in a dressing-gown on Oxford Street. He asked me my birthday, December 21st. He said that I came just between two signs of the Zodiac, Sagittarius and the Goat. I guess I'm both of them at once."

Rocking lightly, tingling like a tray of highballs, the cab jingled. Music came from somewhere—a street piano perhaps—the same old tune, drifting sadly on waves of soft, smoky air; a mendicant melody with no visible means of support. They called to the cabby to follow it, they pursued the vagrant chords down unknown ways of dusk, while London behind them muted its rhythm to a pounding hum. At last they found the minstrel, pulled up beside him, and startled him by their new method of lighting cigarettes.

" I'm still not quite sure of the difference between a half-crown and a florin," he said.

" Then give him both."

When they reached the Serpentine it was too dark to appreciate it.

" Let's bruise it with our heel," she said. " I mean, let's go somewhere. Let's go home, wherever that is."

" Where was it we first met? " He searched his memory. " Long ago. Yes, at that hotel. We'll go back there to tea."

" Is it all right to feel a bit queer in a hansom cab? I mean, almost as though you were on board a ship? I guess I'm worried about my arrow. It doesn't seem to fit as well as it did. My precious arrow. . . ."

His also was trembling strangely. Two lonelinesses must always feel disconcerted when they encounter.

" Darling, darling "; and as she came close into his arms with a queer shudder, the two sparkling darts slipped quietly to the back of the seat.

In the palm room of that hotel is a ceiling of painted mythology. While you wait for anyone who may be coming to have tea with you, you can examine a series of episodes gracefully conjectured from the life of a famous family. First there is Aphrodite, rising alluringly from the foam of a blue sea whose crumbling surf is pink with sunrise. Then there is the marriage, if one calls it so, of Aphrodite and Hephæstus—Vulcan, if you prefer, the fellow the Swedes name their matches after. It was a queer marriage for so handsome a goddess when Aphrodite became the first Mrs. Smith; but handsome women so often choose odd-looking men. Then there's their small boy, Eros, with the toy bow and arrows his father made for him, asking Vulcan to sharpen the darts for him; and his father, busy about thunderbolts, replying that the toys are quite sharp enough. In the last scene Eros, grown to a braw laddie, is trying a chance shot at Psyche. You generally have plenty of time to study all four scenes.

In that hour, late for tea and early for dinner, the palm room was comfortably quiet. The hotel, after the fitful fever of the Atlantic Harmony, slept well. The occasional clink of a teaspoon or a thicker waft of cigarette smoke rising through foliage gave the only trace of what various big game lurked in that jungle. An orchestra groaned softly somewhere far away. It was all so extremely hotel-like, they might just as well have still been on board a ship.

" By the way," he said, " you haven't told me how you happened to go to that lunch."

" Why, it was a young man at the Embassy. He gave me a ticket when I went there to complain about Piccadilly Circus. I mean, about arrows flying around like that. It shouldn't be allowed."

It was at this moment that he noticed the ceiling. It interested him so that he stood up and cricked his neck to see it accurately.

" Have you had all the tea you need? I've

got an idea. There's an errand we ought to do." He carefully picked up the arrows which he had laid under his chair.

The hansom was outside.

" Why, it's still waiting!" she cried. " ' What so proudly we hailed at the twilight's last gleaming.' "

" He must have come back for us. I guess he knows the symptoms."

" The blessed old thing."

" And for all he knew, he might have had to wait till to-morrow."

She made no reply to this, but skipped lightly in. The charioteer leaned indulgently downward, his head on one side, like a dis-illusioned old centaur looking kindly upon the pranks of a couple of young demigods.

" Well, guvner, which way thith time? 'Ampthtead 'eath? "

" We want to go and look at a statue."

" Lord love a duck, guvner, the gallerieth ith clothed."

" The statue in Piccadilly Circus. What do they call it? "

" 'Im? Why that'th Cupid."

They drew up in a side street and crossed the crowded space on foot. Happy as he was, quit of the infernal pang, once more oblivious of terror, mortal loneliness, and dismay, yet the cicatrix of the arrow was still tender. For an instant, as she pressed close beside him,

200

he realized that none of these exquisite moments could be lived again.

The same bobby was directing the traffic; the same imprisoned fires paced like tigers on the roof-tops. The winged boy, tiptoe in jaunty malice, was black against the emerald sky. He pointed to the dainty silhouette of the bow.

"A circus is where one would expect to find sharpshooters," she said.

He climbed past the flower girls, who were arranging their stock of evening boutonnières, and laid the two shining arrows at the base of the frolic statue.

"Here, you dropped something," he said to Eros.

The flower-sellers, shrewdest critics of romance in the most romantic city in the world, held out their nosegays. But the two did not see.

"Well, we're only young once," he said.

"But there's two of us. That makes us young twice."

"I suppose at least we ought to know each other's names."

"It's so much nicer not to."

"Much. Let's be just P and Q."

"P for Psyche?"

"And Q for Cupid."

They walked back to where the cab was waiting.

" Do we have to mind them? " she asked.

" What? "

" Our P's and Q's."

" Hop in, you adorable idiot."

" Where to, guvner? "

" Wherever you please."

" Hullo, it's the same hotel. He thinks we're staying here."

" Maybe he's right."

" But we haven't any baggage. Not even our arrows."

" I can fix that."

" Sorry, guvner, but I'm off. The mare'th earned 'er tea. Will you be goin' out agin to-night? "

" What are you going to tell him? " she asked in sudden panic.

" Nothing. I want to hear you do it."

How delicious her voice was:

" You needn't wait."

REFERRED TO THE AUTHOR

YES, " Obedience " is a fine play. I'm glad they've revived it. Did you know that the first time it was produced, Morgan Edwards played the part of Dunbar? It's rather an odd story.

I never think of Edwards without remembering the dark, creaky stairs in that boardinghouse on Seventy-third Street. That was where I first met him. We had a comical habit of always encountering on the stairs. We would pass with that rather ridiculous murmur and sideling obeisance of two people who don't know each other but want to be polite. I was interested in him at once. Even on the shadowy stairway I could see that he had a fine head, and there was something curiously attractive about his pale, preoccupied face. There was a touch of the unworldly about him and a touch of the tragic too. You know how you divine things about people. " He has troubles of his own " was the banal phrase that came into my mind. Also there was something queerly familiar about him. I wondered if I had seen him before, or only imagined him. I was busy writing, at that time, and my mind was peopled with energetic phantoms. The thought struck me that perhaps he was someone I had invented for a story, but had never given life to. I wondered, was this pale and rather reproachful spectre going to haunt me until the tale was written? At any rate, whatever the story was, I had forgotten it.

One day, as I creaked up the first flight, I saw that he was standing at the head of the stairs, waiting for me to pass. A door was open behind him, and there was light enough to see him clearly. Tall, thin, beautifully shaven on a fine angular jaw that would not be easy to shave, I was surprised to see an air of sudden cheerfulness about him that was almost incongruous. Having thought of him only as a sort of melancholy hallucination living on a dingy stairway, it was quite startling to see him with his face lit up like a lyric poet's, a glow of mundane exhilaration in his eyes. For the first time in our meetings he looked as though to speak to him would not break in upon his secret thoughts. He was the kind of chap, you know, who usually looked as though he was busy thinking. I remember what I said because it was so inane. Some people don't like to cross on the stairs. I looked up as I came to the turn in the steps, and said, " Superstitious?" He smiled and said, "No, I guess not! " " Only in the literal sense, at this moment," I said. An absurd remark, and a horrible pun which I regretted at once, for I thought I would have to explain it. Nothing more humiliating than having to explain a bad pun. But if I didn't explain it, it would seem rude. He looked puzzled, then his face lit up charmingly. " Superstitious—standing above you, eh? I never thought of the meaning before! "

I came up the last steps. " Pardon the vile pun," I said. Then I knew where I had seen him before, and recognized him. " Aren't you Morgan Edwards? " I asked. "Yes," he said.

" I thought so. I remember you in ' After Dinner.' I wrote the notice in the *Observer*. " " By Jove, did you? I *am* glad to meet you. I think that was the nicest thing anyone ever said." His gaunt and pensive face showed a quick flash of that direct and honest friendliness which is so appealing. We found that we were both living on the fourth floor. For similar reasons, undoubtedly. I'm afraid he thought, at first, that I was a dramatic critic of standing. Afterward I explained that the " After Dinner " notice had been only a fluke. I was on the *Observer* when the show was put on, and one of the dramatic men happened to be ill.

Wait a minute: give me a chance! I'll tell it exactly as it came to me, in snips and shreds. At first I didn't pay much attention. I had problems of my own that summer. You know

what a fourth-floor hall bedroom is in hot
weather. I had given up my newspaper job,
and was trying to finish a novel. I couldn't
work late at night, when it was cool, because
if I kept my typewriter going after nine-thirty
the old maid in the next room used to pound
on the partition. I didn't get on very well with
the work, and the money was running low.
Every now and then I would meet Edwards
in the hall. He looked ill and worried, and I
used to think there was a touching pathos in
his careful neatness. My own habits run the
other way—my Palm Beach suit was a wreck,
I remember—but Edwards was always immaculate. I could see—having made it my
business to observe details—how cunningly
he had mended his cuffs and soft collars. Poor
devil! I used to see him going out about noon,
with his cane and Panama hat. I dare say he
scrubbed his hat with his toothbrush. Summer
is a hard time for an actor who hasn't had a
job all spring. Of course there are the pictures,
and summer stock, but I gathered that he had
been ill, and then had turned down several
offers of that sort on account of something
coming along that he had great hopes for. I
remembered his really outstanding work in
" After Dinner," that satiric comedy that fell
dead the winter before. Most of the critics
gave it a good roasting, but knowing what I
do now I expect the real trouble was poor

direction. Fagan was the director, and what did he know of sophisticated comedy? As I say, I had reviewed the piece for the *Observer*, and had been greatly struck by Edwards's playing. Not a leading part, but exquisitely done.

But just at that time I was absorbed in my own not-too-successful affairs. For several years I had been saying to myself that I would do great stuff if I could only get away from the newspaper grind for a few months. And then, when I had saved up five hundred dollars, and buried myself there on Seventy-third Street to write, I couldn't seem to make any headway. I got half through the novel, and then saw that it was paltry stuff. It was flashy, spurious, and raw. One warm evening I was sitting at my window, smoking mournfully and watching some girls who were laughing and talking in a big apartment house that loomed over our lodgings like an ocean liner beside a tugboat. There was a tap at the door. Edwards asked if he could come in. I was surprised, and pleased. He kept very much to himself.

" Glad to see you," I said. " Sit down and have a pipe."

" I didn't want to intrude," he said. " I just wanted to ask you something. You're a literary man. Do you know anything about Arthur Sampson? "

I had to confess that I had never heard the name. No one had, at that time, you remember.

" He's written a play," Edwards said. "A perfectly lovely piece of work. I've got a part in it. By heaven, it seems too good to be true —after a summer like this: illness, the actors' strike, and all that—to get into something so fine. I've just read the whole script. I'm so keen about it, I'm eager to know who the author is. I thought perhaps you might know something about him."

" I guess he's a new man," I said. " What's the play called? "

" 'Obedience.' You know, I've never had such a stroke of luck—it's as if the part had been written for me."

" Splendid! " I said, and I was honestly pleased to hear of his good fortune. " Is it the lead? "

" Oh, no. Of course they want a big name for that. Brooks is the man. My part is only the foil—provides the contrast, you know— on the pay-roll as well as on the stage." He laughed, a little cynically.

" Who's producing it? "

" Upton."

" You don't mean to tell me Upton's got anything good? " I knew little enough about theatrical matters, but even outsiders know Upton's sort of producing, which mostly consists of musical shows where an atrocious libretto is pulled through by an opulent chorus and plenty of eccentric dancing. "A chorus that outstrips them all" was one of his favourite advertising slogans.

"That's why I was wondering about the author Sampson. This must be his first, or he'd never have given it to Upton. Or is Upton going to turn over a new leaf?"

"The only leaves Upton is likely to turn over are fig-leaves," I said brutally. Upton's previous production had been called "The Fig-leaf Lady."

"That's the amazing part of it," said Edwards. "This thing is really exquisite. It is beautifully written: quiet, telling, nothing irrelevant, not a false note. What will happen to it in Upton's hands, God knows! But he seems enthusiastic. He's a likeable cut-throat: let's hope for the best. You're busy—forgive me for breaking in."

Well, of course, some of you have seen "Obedience" since that time, and you know that what Edwards told me was true. The play *was* lovely; not even Upton could kill it altogether. It was Sampson's first. Have any of you read it in printed form? It reads as well as it plays. And the part that Edwards was cast for—Dunbar—is, to any competent spectator, the centre of the action. You remember the lead: the cold, hard, successful hypocrite; and then Dunbar, the blundering, kindly simpleton whose forlorn attempts to create happiness for all about him only succeed in bringing disaster to the one he loves best. It's a great picture of a fine mind and heart, a life of rich, generous possibilities, frittered and wasted and worn out by the needless petty obstinacies of destiny. And all the tragedy (this was the superb touch) because the wretched soul never had courage enough to be unkind. What was it St. Paul, or somebody, said about not being disobedient to the heavenly vision? Dunbar, in the play, was obedient enough, and his heavenly vision made his life a hell. It was the old question of conflicting loyalties. How are you going to solve that?

I suppose the tragic farce is the most perfect conception of man's mind—outside the higher mathematics, I dare say. Everyone knows Sampson's touch now, but it was new then. Some of his situations came pretty close to the nerve-roots. The pitiful absurdity of people in a crisis, exquisite human idiocy where one can't smile because grotesque tragedy is so close . . . those were the scenes that Upton's director thought needed " working up." But I'm getting ahead of my story.

Well, now, let me see. I'd better be a little chronological. It must have been September, because I know I took Labour Day off and went to Long Beach for a swim. I had just about come to the conclusion that my novel was worthless, and that I'd better get a job of some sort. At the far end of the boardwalk, you remember, there's a quiet hotel where one gets away from the crowd, and where you see quite nice-looking people. After I'd had my swim, I thought I'd stroll up that way and have supper there. It's not a cheap place, but I had been living on lunch-counter food all the summer, and I felt I owed myself a little extravagance. I was on my way along the boardwalk, enjoying the cool, strong whiff that comes off the ocean toward sunset, when I saw Edwards, on the other side of the promenade, walking with a girl. My eye caught his, and we raised our hats. I was going on, thinking that perhaps he wasn't so badly off as I had imagined, when to my surprise he ran after me. He looked very haggard and ill, and seemed embarrassed.

" Look here," he said, " it's frightfully awkward: I must have had my pocket picked somehow. I've lost my railroad tickets and everything. Could you possibly lend me enough to get back to town? I've got a lady with me, too."

I didn't need to count my money to know how much I had. It was just about five dollars, and, as you know, that doesn't go far at Long

Beach. I told him how I stood. " I can give you enough for the railroad fares, and glad to," I said. " But how about supper? "

" Oh, we're not hungry," he said; " we had a big lunch." I knew this was probably bravado, but I liked him for saying it. While I was feeling in my pocket for some bills, and wondering how to pass them over to him unobtrusively, he said, " I'd like to introduce you to Miss Cunningham. We're going to be married in the autumn."

You may have seen Sylvia Cunningham? If so, you know how lovely she is. Not pretty, but with the simple charm that beauty can't —— Well, that's trite! She'll never be a great actress, but in the rôle of Sylvia Cunningham she's perfect. I hate to call her slender—it's such an overworked word, but what other is there? Dark hair and clear, amberlucent brown eyes, and a slow, searching way of talking, as if she were really trying to put thought into speech. She, too, poor child, had had a bad summer, I guessed: there was a neat little mend in her glove. She was very friendly—I think Edwards must have told her about that *Observer* notice. I saw that they were both much humiliated at their mishap, and I judged that genial frankness would carry off the situation best.

" Life among the artists! " I said. " What are our assets? "

"I've got seventeen cents," said Edwards. It was a mark of fine breeding, I thought, that he did not insist upon saying how much it was he had lost.

Miss Cunningham began to open her purse. "I have——"

"Nonsense!" I said. "What you have doesn't enter into the audit. In the vulgar phrase, your money's no good. I've got five dollars and a quarter. Now I suggest we go to Jamaica and get supper there, and then go back to town by trolley. It'll be an adventure."

Well, that was what we did, and very jolly it was. You know how it is: artists and actors and manicure girls and newspapermen are accustomed to ups and down of pocket; and when they have a misery in the right-hand trouser they make up for it in a spirit of genial comradeship. Jamaica is an entertaining place. In a little lunch-room, which I remembered from a time when I covered a story out that way, we had excellent ham and eggs, and a good talk.

As we sat in that little white-tiled restaurant I couldn't help watching Edwards. I don't know how to make this plain to you, but our talk, which was cheerful enough, was the least important part of the occasion. Talk tells so little, anyway: most of it's a mere stumbling in an almost foreign tongue when it comes to expressing the inward pangs and certainties that make up life. I had a feeling, as I saw those two, that I was coming closer than ever before to something urgent and fundamental in the human riddle. I thought that I had never seen a man so completely in love. When he looked at her there was a sort of—well, a sort of possession upon him, an enthusiasm, in the true sense of that strange word. I thought to myself that Keats must have looked at Fanny Brawne in just that way. And—you know what writers are—I must confess that my observation of these two began to turn into " copy " in my mind. I was wondering whether they might not give me a hint for my stalled novel.

There are some engaged couples that make it a point of honour to be a bit off-hand and jocose when anyone else is with them. Just to show, I suppose, how sure they are of each other. And somehow I had expected actors, to whom the outward gestures of passion are a mere professional accomplishment, to be a little blasé or polished in such matters. But there was a perfect candour and simplicity about them that touched me keenly. Their relation seemed a lovely thing. Too lovely, and too intense perhaps, to be entirely happy, I thought, for I could see in Edward's face that his whole life and mind were wrapped up in it. I may have been fanciful, but at that time I was seeing the human panorama not for itself but as a reflection of my own amateurish scribblings. In my novel I had been working on the theory—not an original one, of course—that the essence of tragedy is fixing one's passion too deeply on anything in life. In other words, that happiness only comes to those who do not take life too seriously. Destiny, determined not to give up its secrets, always maims or destroys those who press it too closely. As we laughed and enjoyed ourselves over our meal, I was wondering whether Edwards, with his strange air of honourable sorrow, was a proof of my doctrine.

Of course we talked about the new play. Edwards had persuaded Upton to give Miss Cunningham a place in the cast, and she was radiant about it. Her eyes were like pansies as she spoke of it. I remember one thing she said:

" Isn't it wonderful? Morgan and I are together again. You know how much it means to us, for if the show has a run we can get married this winter."

" This fall," Edwards amended.

" Morgan's part is fine," she went on, after a look at him that made even a hardened reporter feel that he had no right to be there. " It's really the big thing in the play for anyone who can understand. It's just made for him."

She was thoughtful a moment, and then

added: "It's *too much* made for him, that's the only trouble. You're living with him, Mr. Roberts. Don't let him take it too hard. He thinks of nothing else."

I made some jocular remark, I forget what. Edwards was silent for a minute. Then he said: "If you knew how I've longed for a part like that—a part that I could really lose myself in."

"I shouldn't care," I said, "to lose myself in a part. Suppose I couldn't find myself again when the time came?"

He turned to me earnestly.

"You're not an actor, Roberts, so perhaps you hardly understand what it means to find a play that's *real*—more real than everyday life. What I mean is this: everyday life is so damned haphazard, troubled by a thousand distractions and subject to every sort of cruel chance. We just fumble along and never know what's coming next. But in a play, a good play, it's all worked out beforehand, you can see the action progressing under clear guidance. What a relief it is to be able to sink yourself in your part, to live it and breathe it and get away for awhile from this pitiless self-consciousness that tags around with us. You remember what they used to say about Booth: that it wasn't Booth playing Hamlet, but Hamlet playing Booth."

The next day, I remember, I tied up my manuscript neatly in a brown paper parcel, marked it *Literary Remains of Leonard Roberts* (I was childish enough to think that the alliteration would please my literary executor, if there should be such a person), put it away in my trunk, and went down to Park Row to see if there were any jobs to be had. Of course it was the usual story. I had been out of the game for six months, and Park Row seemed to have survived the blow with great courage. At the *Observer* office they charitably gave me some books to review. As I came uptown on the subway I was reflecting on the change a few hours had made in my condition. That morning I had been an author, a novelist if you please; and now I was not even a reporter, but that most deplorable of all Grub Street figures, a hack reviewer. It was mid-afternoon, and I hadn't had any lunch yet. In a fit of sulks I went into Browne's, sat down in a corner, and ordered a chop and some shandygaff. As I ate, I looked over the books with a peevish eye. Never mind, I said to myself, I will write such brilliant, withering, and scorching reviews that in six months the Authors' League will be offering me hush money. I was framing the opening paragraph of my first article when Johnson, whom I had known on the *Observer*, stopped at my table. He was one of the newspaper men who had left Park Row to go into professional publicity work. There had been a time when I sneered at such a declension.

" Hullo, Leonard," he said. " What are you doing nowadays? "

I told him, irritably, that I was writing a serial for one of the women's magazines. There is no statement that puts envious awe into a newspaper man so surely as that. But I also admitted that if he knew of a good job I might be persuaded to listen to details.

" As it happens," he said, " I do. Upton, the theatrical producer, is looking for a press agent. He tells me he's got something unusual under way, and he wants a highbrow blurb-artist. He says his regular roughneck is no good for this kind of show. Something by a new writer, rather out of Upton's ordinary line, I guess."

" Is it ' Obedience '? "

" That's it. I couldn't remember the name."

As soon as I had finished my lunch I went round to Upton's office. It was high up in a building overlooking Longacre Square, where the elevators were crowded with the people of that quaint and spurious world. The men I found particularly fascinating—you know the type, so very young in figure, often so old and hard and dry in face, with their lively tweeds, starched blue or green collars, silver-gray ties, and straight-brushed, purply-black hair. It was my first introduction to the realms of theatrical producing, and I must confess that I found Mr. Upton's office very entertaining with its air of elaborate and transparent bunkum. I sat underneath a coloured enlarged photo of the Garden of Eden ballet in "The Fig-leaf Lady" and surveyed the small ante-room. It was all intensely unreal. Those framed photographs, on which were scrawled *To Harry Upton, the Best of his Kind*, or some such inscriptions, and signed by dramatists I had never heard of; the typist pounding out contracts; the architect's drawing of the projected Upton Theatre at Broadway and Fiftieth Street, showing a line of people at the box office—all this, I knew by instinct, meant nothing. The dramatists whose photographs I saw would never write a real play; the Upton Theatre, even if it should be built, would not house anything but "burlettas," and the typed contracts were not worth so much carbon paper. As for Mr. Upton himself, one couldn't help loving him: he was such a disarming, enthusiastic, shrewd, unreliable bandit. To abbreviate, he took me on as a member of his "publicity staff" (consisting of myself and a typewriter, as far as I could see) at one hundred dollars a week. His private office had three ingenious exits; going out by one of them, I found myself in a little alcove with the typewriter and plenty of stationery.

Rehearsals of " Obedience " had started that morning, Upton had told me; so before I went home that afternoon I had typed and sent off the following pregnant paragraph for the next day's papers:

" Henry Upton's first dramatic production of the season, ' Obedience,' by Arthur Sampson, began making elbow room for itself at rehearsals yesterday. Keith Brooks will play the leading rôle, supported by Lillian Llewellyn, Sylvia Cunningham, Morgan Edwards, and other distinguished players."

I had a feeling of cheerfulness that evening. The cursed novel was no longer on my mind, there would be a hundred dollars due to me the next week, and I was about to satisfy my long-standing curiosity to know something about the theatre from the inside. It was one of those typical evenings of New York loveliness: a rich, tawny, lingering light, a dry, clear air, warm enough to be pleasantly soft and yet with a sharp tingle in the breeze. I strolled about that bright jolly neighbourhood round the hideous Verdi statue, bought a volume of Pinero's plays at one of those combination book, cigar, and toy shops, and as I sat in my favourite Milwaukee Lunch I believe (if I must be frank) that some idea of writing a play was flitting through my mind. I got back to my room about ten o'clock. I had just sat down to read Pinero when Edwards tapped at the door. My mouth was open to tell him my surprising news when I saw that he was unpleasantly agitated. First he insisted on returning my loan, although I begged him to believe that there need be no hurry about it.

" Rehearsals began to-day," he said. He sat down on the bed and looked very sombre. " The worst possible has happened," he said. " Fagan's directing."

I tried to console him. Perhaps I felt that if Upton had shown such good sense in his choice of a press representative his judgment in directors couldn't be altogether wrong.

" Oh, well," I said, " if the play's as good as you say, he can't hurt it much. Upton believes in it, he won't let Fagan chop it about, will he? And he's got a good cast— they won't need much direction: they know how to handle that kind of thing."

" It's plain you don't know the game," he said. " If Upton had combed Broadway from Herald Square to Reisenweber's, he couldn't have found a man so superbly equipped to kill the piece. As for poor Sampson, God help him. Fagan is a typical Broadway hanger-on, with plenty of debased cunning of his own; not a fool at all; but the last man for this kind of show, which needs imagination, atmosphere, delicate tone and tempo.

" But that's not all of it. Fagan hates me

223

personally. He'll get me out of the company if he possibly can. He can do it, of course: he has Upton's ear." He sat a moment, one eyebrow twitching nervously. Suddenly he cried out, in a quivering, passionate voice which horrified and frightened me:

" I've *got* to play Dunbar! It's my only chance. *Everything* depends upon it."

Such an outcry, in a man usually so trained, a master of himself, was pitiful. I was truly shocked, and yet I was almost on the verge of nervous laughter, I remember, when the idiotic old spinster in the next room pounded lustily on the wall. I suppose she thought we were revelling. I could see that he needed to talk. I tried to soothe him with some commonplace words and a cigarette.

" No," he said, " I know what I'm talking about. Fagan hates me. No need to go into details. He directed 'After Dinner,' you know —and massacred it. We had a row then . . . he tried to bully a girl in the company . . . I threatened to thrash him. He hasn't forgotten, of course. He passed the word round then that I ruined the show. If this were any other play I'd have walked out as soon as I saw him. But this piece is different. I—I've set my heart on it. My God, I'm just *meant* for that part——"

In the hope of calming him, I asked what had happened at the first rehearsal.

" Oh, the usual thing. We went through the first act, with the sides. I knew my lines perfectly, the only one who did (I ought to, I've been over them incessantly these few weeks—the thing haunts me). That seemed to annoy Fagan. Sampson was there—a quiet little man with a bright, thoughtful eye. For his benefit, evidently, Fagan got off his old tosh about Victor Hugo and the preface to ' Hernani.' It's a bit of patter he picked up somewhere, and uses to impress people with. In the middle of it, he suddenly realized that I had heard it all before. That made him mad. So he cut it short, and reasserted himself by saying that the first act would have to be cut a great deal. Sampson looked pretty groggy, but said nothing. Sampson, I can see, is my only hope. Fagan will try to force me out of the show by hounding me until I lose my temper and quit. He began by telling me how to cross the stage. A man who learned the business under Frank Benson doesn't need to be taught how to walk! "

I ventured some mild sedative opinion, because I saw it did him good to pour out his perplexity.

" You don't know," he said, " how the actor is at the mercy of the director. The director is appointed by the manager and is responsible only to him. If the director takes a dislike to one of the cast, he can tell the manager he ' can't work with him,' and get him fired that way; or he can make the man's position impossible by ridicule and perpetual criticisms at rehearsals. He remarked to-day that I was miscast. The fool! I've never had such a part."

Well, we talked until after midnight, and only stopped then because I was afraid that the spinster might begin to hammer again. In the end I got him fairly well pacified. He was delighted when I told him that I was going to be press agent, and I pleased him by making some memoranda of his previous career, which I thought I could work up into a Sunday story. To tell the truth, I did not, then, take all his distress at its face value. I knew he had had a difficult summer, and was in a nervous, high-strung state. I thought that his trouble was partly what we call " actors' disease," or (to put it more humanely) over-sensitized self-consciousness. I promised to get round to the rehearsal the next day.

As a matter of fact, it was several days before I was able to attend a rehearsal. For the next morning Upton asked me to go to Atlantic City, where he had a musical show opening, to collect data for publicity. His regular press man was ill, and it was evident that he expected me to do plenty of work for my hundred a week. However, it was a new and amusing job, and I was keen to absorb as much local colour as possible. I went to Atlantic city on the train with the " Jazz You Like It " company, took notes of all their life histories, went in swimming with the Blandishing Blondes quartette that afternoon, had them photographed on the sand, took care to see that they were arrested in their one-piece suits, bailed them out, and by dinner-time had collected enough material to fill the trashiest Sunday paper. In the evening the show opened, and I saw what seemed to me the most appallingly vulgar and brutally silly spectacle that had ever disgraced a stage. I wondered how a company of quite intelligent and amusing people could ever have been drilled into such laborious and glittering stupidity. The gallery fell for the Blondes, but the rest of the house suffered for the most part in silence, and I expected to see Upton crushed to earth. When I met him in the lobby afterward I was wondering how to condole with him. To my surprise he was radiant. " Well, I guess we've got a knockout," he said. " This'll sell to the roof on Broadway." He was right, too. Well, this is out of the story. I simply wanted to explain that I was away from New York for several days.

When I got back to Upton's office I was busy most of the day sending out stuff to the papers. Then I asked the imperial young lady who was alternately typing letters and attend-

ing to the little telephone switchboard where
" Obedience " was rehearsing. At the " Stratford," she replied. Wondering how many of
Mr. Upton's amusing and discreditable problems were bestowed under her magnificent
rippling coiffure (she was really a stunning
creature), I went round to that theatre. The
middle door was open and I slipped in. The
house was dark. On the tall naked stage the
rehearsal was proceeding. It was my first
experience of this sort of thing, and I found
it extremely interesting. The stage was set
out with chairs to indicate exits and essentials
of furniture; at the back hung a huge canvas
sea-scene, used in some revue that had opened
at the Stratford the night before. The electricians were tinkering with their illuminating
effects—great blazes and shafts of light criss-
crossed about the place as the rehearsal went
on, much to the annoyance of the actors.
Little electric stars winked in the painted sky
portion of the blue back-drop, and men in
overalls walked about gazing at their tasks.

I sat down quietly in the gloom, about half-
way down the middle aisle. Two or three
other people, whose identity I could not con-
jecture, sat singly down toward the front. In
the orchestra row, in shirtsleeves, with his
feet on the brass rail and a cigar in his mouth,
sat a person who, I saw, must be the renowned
Fagan. Downstage were Brooks, Edwards,

and a charming creature in summery costume who was obviously the original of the multitudinous photographs of Lillian Llewellyn. The rest of the company were sitting about at the back, off the scene. Edwards, who was very pale in the violent downpour of a huge bulb hanging from a wire just overhead, was speaking as I took my seat.

" Wait a minute, folks—*wait a minute!* " cried Fagan sharply. " Now! You've got your situation planted, let's nail it to the cross. Mr. Edwards! "

The actors turned, wearily, and Miss Llewellyn sat down on a chair. Brooks stood waiting with a kind of dogged endurance. At the back of the stage a workman was hammering on a piece of metal. Fagan pulled his legs off the rail and climbed half-way up the little steps leading from the orchestra pit to the proscenium.

" Mr. Edwards! " he shouted, " you're letting it drop. It's dead. Give it to Mr. Brooks so he can pick it up and do something with it. You've got to lift it into the domain of comedy! My God! " he cried, throwing his cigar stub into the orchestra well, " that whole act is terrible. Take it again from Miss Llewellyn's entrance. Mr. Edwards, try to put a little more stuff into it. This isn't amateur theatricals."

Edwards turned as though about to speak,

but he clenched his fist and kept silent. Brooks, however, was less patient.

"Pardon me, Mr. Fagan," he said, in a clear, ironical tone. "But I should like to ask a question, if you will allow me. You speak, very forcibly, of lifting it into the domain of comedy. That seems a curious phrase for this scene. Is it intended to be comic? If so, I must have misconstrued the author's directions in the script."

Brooks was too well known a performer for Fagan to bully. Brooks was " on the lights "— in other words, when the show's electric sign-board went up, it would carry his name. Around his presence hung the mystic aura of five hundred dollars a week, quite enough in itself to make Fagan respectful. The director seemed a little startled by the star's caustic accent. As a matter of fact, I don't suppose he had ever read the script as a whole. I remembered that after the first rehearsal Edwards told me that Fagan had admitted not having read the play. He said he preferred to " pick up the dialogue as they went along." This reference to the author must have seemed to him unaccountably eccentric. I dare say he had forgotten that there was such a person.

He threw up his hands in mock surrender. "All right, all right, if that's the way you take it, I've got nothing to say. Play it your own way, folks. Mr. Edwards, you're killing Mr. Brooks's scene there. Give him time to come down and get his effect."

Again I saw Edwards lift his head as though about to retort, but Brooks whispered something to him. Fagan came back to his seat in the front row and lit a fresh cigar. " Take it from Miss Llewellyn's first entrance," he shouted.

Miss Cunningham and a third man came forward and the five regrouped themselves. The rehearsal resumed. I watched with a curious tingle of excitement. The dialogue meant little to me, plunging in at the middle of the act, but I could not miss the passionate quality of Edwards's playing. Even Brooks, a polished but very cold actor, caught the warmth. Their speeches had the rich vibrance of anger. I was really startled at the power and velocity of the performance, considering that they had only rehearsed a week. As I watched, someone leaned over my shoulder from behind and whispered: " What do you think of Dunbar? "

My eyes had grown accustomed to the gloom. I turned and saw a little man with a thin face and lifted eyebrows which gave him a quaint expression of perpetual surprise. I was so absorbed in the scene that at first I hardly understood.

" Dunbar—? Oh, Edwards? " I whispered. " I think he's corking—fine."

At that moment Edwards was in the middle of a speech. Miss Cunningham had just said something. Edwards, going toward her, had put his hand on her shoulder and was replying in a tone of peculiar tenderness. Fagan's loud voice broke in.

" Dunbar! Mr. Edwards! I can't let you do it like that. You make me hold up this scene every time. Now get it right. This is a bit of comedy, not sob stuff. Try to be a bit facetious, if you can. You're not making love to the girl—not yet!"

There was a moment of silence. Those on the stage stood still, oddly like children halted in the middle of a game. I don't suppose Fagan's words were deliberately intended as a personal insult, but seemed to himself a legitimate comment on the action of the piece. I think his offences came more often from boorish obtuseness than calculated malice. But the brutal interruption, coming after a long and difficult afternoon, strained the players' nerves to snapping. Brooks sat down with an air of calculated nonchalance and took out a cigarette. Then a tinkling hammering began again somewhere up in the flies. Edwards was flushed.

" For God's sake stop that infernal racket up there," he cried. Then, coming down to the unlit gutter of footlights, he said quietly:

" Mr. Fagan, I've studied this part rather

more carefully than you have. If the author is in the house, I'd like to appeal to him as to whether my conception is correct."

There was such a quiver of passion in his voice that even Fagan seemed taken aback.

" What's got into you folks to-day? " he growled. " Oh, very well. Is Mr. Sampson here? "

The little man behind me got up and walked down the aisle in an embarrassed way.

" Mr. Author," said Fagan, " have you been watching the rehearsal? "

Sampson murmured something.

" Is Mr. Edwards doing the part as you want it done? "

" Mr. Edwards is perfectly right," said Sampson.

" Thank you, sir," said Edwards from the stage. " Fagan, when you are ready to conduct rehearsals like a gentleman, I will be here." He turned and walked off the stage.

Brooks snapped his cigarette-case to, and the sharp click seemed to bring the scene to an end. Fagan picked up his coat from the seat beside him. " Bolshevism! " he said. " All right, folks, ten o'clock to-morrow, here. Miss Cunningham, will you tell Mr. Edwards ten o'clock to-morrow? "

This last might be taken either as a surly apology, or as an added insult. Rather subtle for Fagan, I thought. As I was getting out of

my seat, the director and a venomous-looking
young man whom I had seen in and out of
Upton's office walked up the aisle together.
Sampson was just behind them. I could see
that the director was either furiously angry
or else (more likely) deemed it his duty to
pretend to be.

"This show's no good as long as Edwards
is in it," he said loudly, spitting out fragments of cigar-wrapper. "That fellow's
breaking up the company. I sha'n't be able
to handle 'em at all, pretty soon. This kind
of thing puts an omen on a show."

Well, that was my introduction to "Obedience." I watched Fagan and the hanger-on
of Upton's office—one of those innumerable
black-haired young infidels who run errands
for a man like Upton, hobnob with the ticket
speculators in the enigmatic argot of the box
office, and seem to look out upon the world
from behind a little grill of brass railings.
They moved up the velvet slope of the passage,
arguing hoarsely. Sampson faded gently away
into the darkness and disappeared through
the thick blue curtains of the foyer. An idea
struck me, and I ran behind to see the stage
manager, Cervaux, who was playing one of
the minor parts. I cajoled his own copy of the
script away from him, promising to return it
to the office the next morning. I wanted to

read the play entire. Going out toward the stage door, behind a big flat of scenery I came upon Miss Cunningham. She was sitting in a rolling chair, one of those things you see on the boardwalk at Atlantic City. There was a whole fleet of them drawn up in the wings, they were used in that idiotic revue playing at the Stratford. It added to the curiously unreal atmosphere of the occasion to see her crouching there, crying, alone in the half-light, among those absurd vehicles of joy.

I intended to pass as though I hadn't seen her, but she called out to me. If Upton could have seen her then, her honey-brown eyes glazed with tears, black rings in her poor little pale face, he would have raised her salary—or else fired her, I don't know which.

" Mr. Roberts," she said, slowly and tremulously—" I don't know who else to ask. Will you try to help Morgan? "

" Why, of course," I said. " Anything I can do——"

" You were at the rehearsal? Then you saw how Fagan treats him. It's been like that every day. The brute! It's abominable! You know how we had set our hearts on playing this together, Morgan and I. . . . Now I've almost come to pray that Morgan will throw it up. That's what Fagan wants, of course, but I don't care. All I want is his happiness. I said something to him about giving up the

part, but he—— Mr. Roberts, I'm *worried*.
I've never seen Morgan so strange before.
He's not himself. I don't know what's the
matter, I have a feeling that something——"

The electricians were still fooling about
with their spotlights, and a great arrow of
brilliance sliced across the stage and groped
about us. It blazed brutally upon her tear-
stained face, and then see-sawed among the
little flock of rolling chairs. It was that shaft
of light that dispelled, once for all, the feeling
I had had that this was all some sort of
theatrical gibberish, pantomime stuff intended
to impress the greenhorn press agent. For
when she recoiled under the blow of that
sudden stroke of brightness I could read un-
questionable trouble on her face. There was
not only perplexity, there was fear.

She was silent, turning her face away. Then
she stepped down from the chair, in a blind
sort of way.

" I begged him to give it up," she said
quietly. " He said that no one but the author
could take him out of this part. I wish the
author would.—Oh, I don't know what to
wish! Morgan's making himself ill fighting
against Fagan."

We walked across Fortieth Street together,
and I escorted her as far as a Fifth Avenue
bus. As we waited for the bus she said:

" You'll probably see him to-night. Tell

him about rehearsal to-morrow, ten o'clock. He had gone before I could speak to him. You see, he's not himself. We were to have taken supper together."

She added something that I have never forgotten:

"The worst tragedy in the world is when lovely things get in the hands of people who don't understand them. If you see Mr. Sampson, you might tell him that. Some day he may write another play."

When I got up to Seventy-third Street I tapped at Edwards's door. He was at his table, writing. I had intended to ask him to take dinner with me, thinking that perhaps I could help him, but his manner showed plainly that he wanted to be alone. If I had been an old friend of his, perhaps I could have done something, but I did not feel I knew him well enough to force myself upon his mood.

"Fagan sent you word, rehearsal to-morrow at ten," I said. "It sounds to me like an apology."

He looked at me steadily.

"You were there to-day? You will understand a little, then."

"I understand that Fagan is a ruffian."

"Fagan—oh, I don't mean Fagan." He paused and looked at the wet point of his pen. "I was just writing a note to Sampson," he said. He hesitated a moment, and then tore

237

the written sheet across several times and
dropped it in the basket.

"Oh, hell!" he said. "I can't appeal to
Sampson again. I'll have to work it out myself.—Don't imagine I take Fagan too
seriously. Fagan is only an accident. A tragic
accident. That's part of my weird, as the
Scotch say. I mean, you'll understand better
about Dunbar."

I didn't quite understand, and said nothing.

"I wouldn't let a man like Fagan stand
between me and Dunbar," he said. "It's in
the hands of the author now. You heard what
he said. He put Dunbar into the play, he's
the only one who can take him out of it."

The next morning Upton broke the news
to me that I was to go out as advance man.
The opening was set for Providence, only ten
days later. There was to be a two-weeks tour
of three-night engagements, and I had to
arrange for the publicity, poster-printing, ac-
commodations for the company and so one.
This did not appeal to me very strongly, but
I scrambled together a lot of photographs,
interviewed the cast as to their preferences in
hotel rooms, and set off. I got back a week
later. We were then only three days away from
the opening. They were rehearsing with the
sets, Upton's telephone blonde told me, and
I hurried round to the Stratford to see how
the scenic artist had done the job.

They had just knocked off for lunch when I got there, and at the stage door I met Edwards coming out with Miss Cunningham. He looked very white and tired.

" Hullo," I said; " just in time to have lunch with me! Come on, we'll go to Maxim's. I've still got some of Upton's expense money."

" I've got to rush round to the modiste for a fitting," said Miss Cunningham. " The gowns are just finished. You take Morgan and give him a good talking-to. He needs it." I did not quite understand the appeal in her eyes, but I saw that she wanted me to talk with Edwards alone. She went toward Bryant Park, and we turned down to Thirty-eighth. Edwards stood a moment at the corner looking after her.

" Sylvia says I'm a fool," he said wearily. " I don't know: most of us are, one way or another.—You know I told you that I put my confidence in the author."

" Quite right," I said. " I myself heard Sampson say he thought you were corking."

" Well, I wonder if he's double-crossing me? " said Edwards slowly, as though to himself.

" In what way? "

" Yesterday, when I was coming down to rehearsal, there was a tie-up of some kind on the subway. The train stood still for a long time, and then the lights went out. We stayed

in the dark for I don't know how long—
everybody got nervous. It was pitch black,
and awfully hot and stuffy. The women began
to scream. I felt pretty queer myself—you
know I haven't been well—and as we sat
there I went off into a kind of doze or something. Then, just as everybody was on the
edge of a panic, the lights came on and we
went ahead. When we got to Times Square I
think I must have been a bit off colour, for
the damned rehearsal went out of my head
entirely. Suddenly I realized I was in a drug-
store drinking some headache fizz when I
was over an hour late at the theatre. My God!
I hustled down there as fast as I could go.
Queer thing. I went in through the stage
door, and as I came round behind the set I
heard voices on the stage. They were rehearsing, of course. Naturally, they couldn't
wait all morning for me. But this is what I'm
getting at. You know that scene in the second
act where I say to Brooks:

> It's all very well for you to say that, Ah, hah!
> I see! But suppose you had been in my place—

You know that's a turning point in the
act. There's a particular inflection I give that
speech—the way I say the ' Ah, hah! I see! '
that makes the point clear to the audience and
gets it over. Well, they were rehearsing that
scene, and from behind the canvas I heard

that speech. And what I heard was *my own voice.*"

" What on earth do you mean? " I said.

He hesitated. He was sitting, his lunch almost untasted, with one elbow on the table and his forehead leaning on his hand. Under his long, sinewy fingers I could see his brows tightened and frowning downward upon his plate.

" Exactly what I say. It was my own voice. Or, if you prefer, Dunbar's voice. I heard that speech uttered, tone for tone, as I had been saying it. It was the precise accent and pitch of ironical comment which I had thought appropriate for Dunbar at that point in the action. The sudden change of tone, the pause, the placing of the emphasis—the words were just as if they had come out of my own mouth. I stopped, instinctively. I said to myself, has Fagan got someone else to play the part, and been coaching him on the side? Someone who's been sitting in at rehearsals and has picked up my conception of Dunbar? And at that moment I heard Fagan sing out ' All right, folks, the carpenter wants to work on this set. We'll quit until after lunch.'

" I tell you, I was staggered. If I was out, I was out, but they might have been straight with me. It was a matter for the Equity, I thought. I didn't want to chin it over with the others just then, and I heard them coming off, so I slipped through the door that opens into the passage behind the stage-box. I meant to tell Fagan what I thought about it. There was Sampson sitting in one of the boxes. He saw me, and got up. He said: 'By Jove, Mr. Edwards, you were fine this morning. I've never seen you do it so well. It was bully, all through. Keep it like that, and you're the hit of the play.'

" I thought at first he was making fun of me. I was about to make some sarcastic retort, when he put out his hand in the friendliest way, and said:

" ' I want to thank you for what you're doing for that part, and I know it hasn't been easy. I've never seen anything so beautifully done, and just want to tell you that if the play is a success it will be largely due to you.'

" This, on the heels of the other, astounded me so that I didn't know what to say. I made some automatic reply, and he left. I sat down in the cool darkness of the box to rest, for I was feeling very seedy. My head went round and round—touch of the sun, I dare say, or that foul air in the crowded subway car. I was still there when they came back, an hour later, for the afternoon rehearsal. I tried to talk to Sylvia about it, but all she would say was that I ought to go to a doctor."

" I think she's right," I said. " Look here, have you had any sleep lately? "

" You seem to have forgotten Dunbar's line," he said. " ' *There'll be plenty of time to sleep by and by.* ' "

" For God's sake forget about Dunbar," I said. " Man, dear, you're on the tip of a nervous breakdown. Now listen. This is Friday. Dress rehearsal to-morrow. Sunday you'll have all day off. Take Miss Cunningham and go away into the country somewhere and rest. Put the damned play out of your mind and give her a good time. You both need it."

I didn't see him again until Monday morning. I went up to Providence on the train with the company. As I passed through one of the Pullmans looking for a seat in a smoking compartment, I found Miss Cunningham and Edwards sitting in adjoining chairs. To my delight they seemed very cheerful, and smiled up at me charmingly.

" Took your advice yesterday," he said. " We went down to Long Beach again. Had a lovely day, not even a pickpocket to spoil it."

" What an unfortunate remark! " said Sylvia, laughing. " He means, not a pickpocket to bring us a friend in need and give us a jolly evening in Jamaica."

" I spoke the speech trippingly," he admitted.

" And we left Dunbar behind! " said

Sylvia. She flashed me a grateful little look that showed she knew I had tried to help.

" Have you decided where to spend the honeymoon? " I asked, greatly pleased to see them so happy.

" Hush! " she said. " We'll wait till we see what sort of notices the show gets."

" Think of the poor press agent. I've used up all my dope. Get spliced while we're in Providence and it'll give me a nice little story. You know the kind of thing—' CRITICS' PRAISE BRINGS PAIR TO ALTAR; PRESS CLIPPINGS CUPID'S AID.' "

" You're getting as vulgar as a regular press agent," she said merrily. " They don't think of anything except in terms of good stories for the paper."

" Oh," I said, " the press agent has his tragedies, too. Think how many stories he knows that he can't tell."

I felt that this remark was not very happily inspired, and went on through the car calling myself a clumsy idiot. In the smoking compartment, as luck would have it, were both Upton and Fagan, smoking huge cigars and talking together. I sat down and lit my pipe. Fagan, in his usual way, was trying to impress Upton with his own sagacity. There was another musical horror of Upton's scheduled to begin rehearsal shortly, and probably Fagan was hoping to land the job as director.

" What did you think of Edwards at the dress rehearsal ? " said Fagan.

Upton grunted. He had a way of retaining his ideas until others had committed themselves.

" I've been telling you right along, he's impossible," said Fagan. " No one can work with him. He's too damned upstage. Now I got Billy Mitford to promise he'd run up and see the opening. Billy is the man you need for that part. I had him in at the dress, and he'll be there to-night. I've given him a line on the part, and if Edwards falls out we can start rehearsing Billy right away. He could get set in a week, and open with the show in New York."

" Four hundred a week," was Upton's comment, seemingly addressed to the end of his cigar.

" All right, he's worth it. He's got a following. This guy Edwards is dear at any price. He'll kill the show. He doesn't get his stuff over. God knows I've worked on him. And he crabs Brooks's work more'n half the time. What you want is one of these birds that gets the women climbing over the orchestra rail. Billy is your one best bet, take it from me."

" Well, we'll open her up and see what we got," said Upton. " Is Sampson along ? "

" No. Scared. Said he was too nervous to come. He'll learn to write a play afterwhile.

What a mess that script was until I got her straightened out."

When we got to Providence I had several jobs to do around town. I visited the newspaper offices, stopped in at the theatre where the stage crew were busy unloading scenery, and when I returned to the hotel I lay down in my room and had a good nap. I was awakened late in the afternoon—about five o'clock, because I looked at my watch—by a knocking at the door. I got up and opened. It was Edwards. To my dismay, his cheerfulness had vanished. He had gone back to the old pallid and anxious mood.

" Nervous, old man? " I said. When I had booked the rooms for the company I had arranged that he and I should be next door to each other, so that I could keep an eye on him.

" Nervous? " he said. " I'm ill. Had another of those damned swimming spells in my head. Haven't got any brandy, have you? "

I hadn't, but offered to go in search of some. He wouldn't let me.

" Don't go," he said. " Look here, I saw Mitford in the lobby just now. What the devil is he doing here? "

" Perhaps there's some other show on," I suggested miserably.

" I told you they were trying to double-cross me," he said. " I know perfectly well

246

what he's here for. Fagan is trying to razz me into a breakdown. Then he'll put Mitford in as Dunbar. But I tell you, I'll play this thing in spite of hell and high water."

He paced feverishly up and down, and I tried to ease his mind.

" By God, they shan't! " he cried. " I'll put this thing up to the author. Where's Sampson? "

"He's not here. For Heaven's sake, man, don't get in a state. Everything's all right."

" Everything's all right! " he repeated bitterly. " Yes, everything's lovely. Let's ' lift it into the domain of comedy.' But if you see Fagan, tell him to keep away from me."

I begged him to rest until dinner-time. I went into his room with him, made him lie down on the bed, rang for a bottle of ice water, and left him there. Then I went downstairs and wrote a couple of letters. I was just leaving the hotel when I met Fagan coming in. He stopped me to ask if I had taken care to put his name on the playbill as director. I had. If the show was a flop, I at least wanted his name attached as a participial cause.

I wandered uneasily about the busy streets until theatre time. I couldn't have been more nervous if I had been going on the boards myself. I spent part of the time prowling about trying to see how much " Obedience " paper I could find on the billboards and in shop windows. I stepped in at a lunch-room and had some supper. The place reminded me of the little café in Jamaica where Sylvia and Edwards and I had eaten together. My mind was full of the picture of the two, and his face as he leaned across the table toward her. I thought that I had never seen a couple who so deserved happiness, or who had fought harder to earn it. What was the subtle appeal in this play that made it react so strangely upon him? The tragedy of Dunbar in the piece, the sacrifice of the poor, well-meaning fellow whose virtue always seemed to turn and rend him, did this echo some secret experience in his own life? I wondered whether an actor's career was really the gay business I had conceived it. It occurred to me that perhaps the actor's profession is doomed to suffering, because it takes the most dangerous explosives in life and plays with them. Love, ambition, jealousy, hatred, those are the things actors deal with. You can't play with those without one of them going off every now and then. They go off with a bang, and somebody gets hurt.

I suppose I'm sentimental. I wanted those two to win out. It seemed to me that a defeat for their fine and honourable passion would be a defeat for Love everywhere, and for all who believe in the worthy aspirations of the heart. I don't suppose any press agent ever pondered more generous philosophies than I did that night, over my lunch-counter supper.

Time went so fast that it was after eight when I got to the theatre. I went in and took a seat in the last row. The house, to my surprise, was crowded. I could see Upton's big bald head, well down in front, beside a massively carved lady, all bust and beads, whom I supposed to be Mrs. Upton. The élite of Providence were out in force, for Brooks's name is always a drawing card. Some of them, I feared, were going to be disappointed. It is all very well to introduce a new Barrie or a new Pinero to the playgoing public, but you've got to remember that it is bound to be grievous for those who prefer the other sort of thing.

The curtain, of course, was late, and I gave a sigh of relief when I saw it go up. Edwards, waiting carefully for the hush, had the house with him in three speeches. I have never seen better work, before or since. It was noticeable that at his first exit he got a bigger hand than Brooks at his carefully prepared entrance. The only thing that seemed to me out of the way was his extreme pallor. The silly ass, I said to myself, he hasn't made himself up properly. Then it struck me that it was probably a sound touch of realism, for certainly Dunbar would not be described as a full-blooded creature. I had read the play carefully, and had seen it in rehearsal; but I had never known how much there was in it. Strangely enough, Edwards was the only one who showed no trace of nervousness. All the others, even Brooks, seemed unaccountably at a loss now and then, trampled on their lines, and smothered their points. At first the house was inclined to applaud, but as the action tightened, they hushed into the perfect and passionate silence that is the playwright's dream. There were six curtains at the end of the first act. I could tell by the tilt of old Upton's pink pate that he was in fine spirits. I looked about for Fagan in the lobby, as I was keen to see how he was taking it, but missed him in the arguing and shifting crowd.

By the time the third act was underway it was plain that we had a sure-fire success. Novice as I was, I could read the signs when I saw Upton scribbling telegrams at the box-office window in the second intermission, and observed the face of Mr. Mitford. The usual slips that always happen on first nights were there, of course. In the third act, when Edwards had to take Sylvia in his arms, she seemed to trip and almost fell; and I noticed that Brooks crossed the stage and helped her off, which was not in the script; but these things were not marked by most of the audience. Dunbar, you remember, makes his final exit several minutes before the end of the third act. When he went off there was a little stir among the audience—far more eloquent than applause would have been. That beautiful delineation of a blundering high-minded failure had made its appeal.

After Edwards's last exit I felt my way out, quietly, and went round through the street and up the alley to the stage door. I wanted to be the first to congratulate him on his splendid triumph. I did not want to break in too soon, so I waited near the door until I heard the crash of hands that followed the curtain. The canvas rose and fell repeatedly as the players took their calls, while the house shook with applause. From where I stood, by the switches and buttons on the control board, I could see them lined up in the orange glare of the gutter, bowing and smiling. There were cries of " Dunbar! Dunbar! " and a rumbling of feet in the gallery. It is the only time I have ever seen an audience crowd down the aisles and stand by the orchestra rail, applauding. Then I saw why they lingered. Edwards had not taken his call.

The curtain fell again, and Cervaux, the stage manager, came running off, the perspiration streaming down over his grease-paint.

" Christ! " he cried. " Where's that fool Edwards? "

As soon as the curtain finally shut off the

house I could see the actors turn to each other as though in dismay. Miss Cunningham came off, and I ran to shake her hand. To my amazement she looked at me blankly, with a dreadful face, and sat down on a trunk.

Brooks strode across the stage. " Where's Edwards? " he shouted angrily. " Tell him to take this call with me, the house is crazy."

" Where's the author? " said someone. " They want the author too."

Several hurried upstairs to the men's dressing-rooms, and I followed. The door of number 3, on which Edwards's name was scrawled in chalk, stood open. Cervaux stood stupidly on the sill. The room was empty.

" He's gone," said Cervaux. " What do you know about that? "

We could still hear the tumult of the house.

" Take the curtain, Mr. Brooks," said Cervaux. " Tell them he's ill."

I looked round number 3 dressing-room.

There was a taxi standing outside the stage door. I don't know how it happened to be there, or who had ordered it, but I shouted to the driver and jumped in. I have a faint impression that just as the engine started Sylvia appeared at the door, with a cloak thrown over her stage gown, and cried something, but I am not sure.

When I got to the hotel, the door of the room next to mine was locked, but the house detective got it open without any noise. There were two men in the room. In the far corner lay Fagan, unconscious, with a broken jaw, one arm hideously twisted under him, and a shattered water bottle beside his bloody head. Sprawled against the bed, kneeling, with his arms flung out across the counterpane, was Edwards.—The doctor said it was heart disease. He had been dead since six o'clock.

The Westminster Press
411a Harrow Road
London, W.9